BEGINNING

IN

1861

A NOVEL OF THE
WAR BETWEEN THE STATES

Jay Davis, Jr.

FITHIAN PRESS, SANTA BARBARA, 1994

To Sylvia,
the best in my life
the light of my life.

Copyright © 1994 Jay Davis, Jr.
All Rights Reserved
Printed in the United States of America

Published by Fithian Press
A division of Daniel and Daniel, Publishers, Inc.
Post Office Box 1525
Santa Barbara, CA 93102

Design: Eric Larson
Set in Janson

LIBRARY OF CONGRESS CATALOGING-IN-PUBLICATION DATA
Davis, Jay
    Beginning in 1861 : a novel of the War between the States / Jay Davis.
        p.   cm.
    ISBN 1-56474-108-7
    1. United States—History—Civil War, 1861-1865—Fiction.
I. Title
PS3554.A93475B4   1994
81e'.54—dc20   94-16389
                                                    CIP

Contents

Preface

History is often taught in a cruel manner; names, dates, who won, and the number of men lost. This book tells the story of the War between the States (Civil War) through the words, thoughts and actions of the people who lived through a stressful time in our nation's history. Twelve years of research have been used to make the story real in terms of where the people were and what they did. Some of the findings have not been reported before or have not been frequently mentioned, especially in reference to Lee, Davis, Summers, Brooks, Tyler, etc.

The story takes a sixteen-year-old husky boy, his companion and his grandfather through the family stress and the nation's stress during the war and the post-war adjustment period. This is what happened to the people in Prince Edward County, Virginia, beginning in 1861.

CHAPTER I

Virginia, April 1861

"MACON take my gun, while I show the dog what he is to do when he hears a two-note whistle. Keep a sharp eye out for the squirrel and get him in the head when he comes around the tree. There is a hair-trigger on my new rifle. Grandfather had a light trigger made for it; do not put your finger inside the guard until you have the squirrel in the sights. Get his head in the sights and we will have fried squirrel for our dinner."

Dan turned and walked to the tree and grabbed the dog's collar; using a two-tone whistle he worked the dog around the tree. As Dan and the dog moved, the squirrel moved to keep the tree as a buffer. Macon got a bead on the squirrel's head, reached into the trigger guard and the gun fired without his being aware he had pulled the trigger. The squirrel tumbled to the ground as Macon stared at the gun, not believing he really had pulled the trigger.

"Master Dan that thing is dangerous. I hardly touched the gun and it fired."

Dan said, "Look at the squirrel. You got him right in the head. That's the reason Grandpa Johns had the trigger honed for a light touch. You don't pull off the target as you squeeze the trigger."

"Maybe this pup will learn to go around the tree when he hears my two-tone whistle. Anyway Macon, we have a good squirrel for

Kitty to fix for dinner. Be sure you clean the gun before you put it in the rack. Don't say anything about firing my gun because I would get in trouble with my dad if he knew I let a slave learn how to shoot. You remember the strapping I got when he caught me showing you how to write your name.

"Macon, it seems to me that April in Virginia is something special. Everything grows so fast, smells so good, the air is so balmy, and the skies so blue that this must make a treasured place in the world. We better get on home; Kitty will need time to cook the squirrel for dinner."

As they cleared the creek and the trees, they could see the home place. Macon was the first to spot two horses at the rail. "Looks like we got company; one of them is your grandfather Johns; don't know who the other one is."

Dan looked at the horses, recognized his grandfather's mare but did not know the other animal, a massive gray. Then he noticed the saddle blanket bore a Virginia volunteer's insignia.

"It has to be my half brother, Tom. It will be great to see him again."

"Tom is your father."

"That is true and my half brother is Thomas, Jr."

"Just like your name is Dan and your grandfather's name is Daniel Johns."

"Almost the same."

"How come my mom, Kitty and I live here with the Woottons but we belong to your grandfather Johns?"

"I will explain that to you some day. Give the squirrel to Kitty and clean the rifle good." As Dan turned to go up the steps, his mother opened the front door and motioned for him to be quiet. She came down the steps and waited for Macon to get out of sight.

"Dan you missed your lessons today. The tutor stayed while he could this morning and then had to leave to make his other schedule. Your father and I are very angry about you wandering off and no one ever knows where you have gone. Your father is furious but we have company as you can see and we do not need a scene. Go around back and use the back stairs to get to your room and get cleaned up for dinner. We want you here in the house until tomorrow morning when we will discuss what you must do to remember your lessons and studies. You will want to see Tom and your grandfather and do not cross your father. He will be struggling to contain himself and we must not spoil Tom's visit with his father. Tom's troop is ready to be dispatched and we may not see him as often as we'd like. He has to go back home tomorrow morning."

"I'm sorry, Mom. I just forgot. Macon and I had to get the new dog trained and I forgot it was class day, I'm sorry."

"I know you are Dan but you must understand your father considers knowing Greek and Latin is necessary for a gentleman to deal with life. You may not agree or understand at this time because at sixteen, most people know they are ready to conquer the world. It is only after a few years have passed that they wonder why they did not make better use of their time."

Dan turned to the back of the house, stopping at the wash rack alongside the kitchen where Macon was cleaning the rifle.

Macon said: "This sure is a fancy rifle."

Dan replied, "Grandpa Johns got two of these new Spencers, one for himself and one for me. They are the greatest guns I have ever seen. Having cartridge instead of having to fuss with ball and powder is a lot more fun."

Dan finished washing and entered the kitchen to take the back stairs to his room. Kitty was preparing drinks for the people in the parlor and turned to Dan as he started up the stairs, "You better hurry cause you are missing the discussions of the crisis and you know how much you want to know what is happening."

Dan said, "Yes, I know and I'm also in the doghouse for missing my lessons. You and Macon have the squirrel for dinner. I better not do anything to draw attention to young Dan today. If father is celebrating, I'm in for a rough session today or tomorrow. I'll change clothes and be right down."

A few minutes later Dan entered the parlor to be greeted by his father, "Well here is our lost son. Say hello to Tom and Grandpa Johns."

"Hello Tom. What a great uniform. You are impressive. Are you ready to report for duty?"

"Good to see you, Dan. You sure have filled out since I have seen you. Yes, the Virginia legislature has authorized the establishment of three armories and I'm charged with getting one of them started."

"How about taking me with you."

"You know I would like to have you, Dan. You know guns because you grandfather has taught you about them ever since you were old enough to shoot but you must be at least eighteen years old to get into the Virginia Volunteers. I expect you would be a better man than some I will have and you have grown; you could pass for eighteen or nineteen but too many people know us here in Virginia. The colonel would boot both of us out of the service or worse. For now, you should be here with your family helping your father and grandfather run these places."

"You're probably right, but I sure don't want to be left out of the things. Hello Grandpa, glad you could come over. Hello, Dad. Sorry I'm late."

"Did your mother tell you about tomorrow?"

"Yes Father, I understand."

"Good. Tom, what do you hear about the Virginia compromise around Richmond?"

"Dad, the general impression is we should try but the people in Washington don't want a compromise. What do you think, Mr. Johns?"

"Tom, I think there are enough people in Congress who smell a chance to grab power since nine states have left the Union. With eighteen senators out of key spots, this leaves openings for the radicals to grab power. I've never known a politician to reject a chance for power or agree to give it up once he has it in his hands.

I'm sure our delegation has made some progress but I don't think they can prevail against the radicals left in charge. This is the practical result of the ideas Yancy and his kind have sold to the cotton states. It's too bad things are this way. I'm afraid we have some idiots on both sides."

"Didn't President Tyler present his case direct to President Buchanan?" young Tom asked.

"The *Richmond Despatch* reported he did and from others I understand he had a long private session with Buchanan. Tyler has done yeoman service for the Union; he has highlighted the problem and carried the day in getting the framework together to solve the problem. Tyler cannot give the order to convene the commissioners; the president has to do that. Buchanan may be one of those who stood there when the Lord was passing out brains and thought the Lord said trains. He should understand and can act but he has doomed the effort to failure by writing to Congress urging they do something because he doesn't believe he has the power to act. His letter states he 'hails this movement by Virginia with great satisfaction' and then says he does not have the power to make the appointments. The last time anyone did this, he washed his hands."

Tom Sr. interrupted to ask, "Martha, would you have Kitty make another round of drinks." He turned back to his father-in-law, "What do you think that Governor Pickens will do now that they have turned away the relief ship, the *Star of the West?*"

"I'm sure you know Pickens is not in control. He sneezes whenever one of a dozen or more people take snuff. I think we will be very lucky if we manage without some of those hotheads like Yancy firing on the flag. There have been ample grounds for calling some past acts an insurgence. Maybe because they have not, the Yancy-Pickens gang think they can do whatever they wish to do to bluff the Union into concessions. I don't think Lincoln can be bluffed and I don't think anyone can fire on the flag without starting a real war."

Tom Sr. asked, "What do you think Virginia will do if war breaks out?"

"I hope there's some way found for Virginia to stay out of the conflict and be a factor in causing a solution to our increasingly bitter sectional quarrels. Several other states, I'm sure feel the same way but I'm not betting we will be that lucky."

Martha announced, "Kitty has dinner ready and we better postpone the discussions if we want the food, while it is hot. Kitty has done her best to make chicken and dumplings just the way you like them, Father."

As they went into the dining room, Daniel Johns hugged his daughter and said, "You'll always be my favorite child, Martha."

"How you do kid, Sir. Since I'm your only child I have to work very hard to get you to make that declaration. Do sit down and enjoy your meal."

The four males made short work of Kitty's chicken dish and then were served the green salad. When Tom Sr. tasted his salad he felt grit.

He called to Kitty, "I wish you would take better care with washing the greens."

And Kitty replied, "Mr. Wootton every man has to eat his peck of dirt."

Tom Sr. responded, "Not all once, datshamet."

Martha broke in with, "You men take your coffee and brandy here at the table and I will talk to Kitty."

Tom Jr. turned to his father, "Dad will you try to go back into the service if war breaks out?"

"Son I doubt anyone would give me a command after the quarrel I had in the '45 campaign and I don't know how my health would hold up in a field assignment. You know I don't think Jeff Davis is the best man the South could have picked and I'm sure he will remember our last meeting."

"What do you think Lee will do? The rumor has it Scott will offer him command of the army."

"I doubt Scott will because he doesn't want to step down but Lincoln and his advisors will shift Scott aside and make Lee an offer. Lee doesn't believe in the secession movement any more than Mr. Johns does but he will not fight against the South. My guess is he'll do nothing unless Virginia leaves the Union. He wouldn't be Jeff Davis' first choice for command but he's by far the best man for the job."

Tom Jr. asked his father, "Why would Davis want someone other than Lee to head the Confederate army?"

"These appointments are always more political than trying to get the best man. Davis knows he has the best military mind in the South. I may be prejudiced but I know both men and I know others who agree with me that Davis can be the South's downfall."

Daniel Johns broke in, "You are exactly right there and everyone knows you and I don't always agree."

Tom Jr. turned back to his father, "Many people think if war comes it'll be a short war, say six months. What do you think?"

"Yancy and his group have been selling this as a part of his hypothesis that the North will back down. I just don't believe it is true. Civil conflicts have a way of dragging out and usually result in horrible cruelty. Cromwell's exploits are a good example of this. Anything is possible in war, there always are bizarre situations developing and sometimes great victories develop from just such conditions but to count on that happening shortly after war breaks out is really foolish. I think I'll go upstairs and have a nap if you'll help me get to my room, Tom.

Tom Jr. helped his father to his room and pulled off his boots and folded his jacket as Senior stretched out on the bed. As he returned to the ground floor, Dan and his grandfather were ready to go down the steps to the horses.

"Are you leaving, Mr. Johns?"

"I should get on home, Tom. I'm constructing some new barns and I'm anxious to see them finished. I have supplies ordered that could be here next month. Anyway, you and Dan will have many things to discuss. I'll try to get back here before you leave tomorrow morning."

"Good-by Grandpa. See you tomorrow," said Dan as his grandfather cantered off.

Dan turned towards Tom's horse and said, "Tom, what a great horse you have. When did you get him?"

"I traded for him last month. I didn't put him in the barn because I wanted you to see him and get a chance to ride him. Slip on these spurs and give him a walk out to the big tree and then give him his head for the run back." Dan sprang into the saddle and turned the horse in the direction of the tree, trying the horse's response to the reins on the way out. As they turned around, Dan lifted the reins and touched the spurs to the horse's flank. The gray responded with a surge that might have unseated a less skilled rider. The power and speed of the gray made Dan feel like he was flying. All too soon, he was at the house and he had to rein the gray to a stop.

"Tom, this is the greatest horse I ever rode. Grandpa's mare is a pleasure to ride and can do many things but this guy has great brute power. You feel like he could go forever and over anything. Why did they geld him? They should have used him to breed more like him."

"Dan, no one could control him as a stud and the only way they could get anything done with him was as a gelding. He is really great."

"He sure is. Let's walk him on down to the barn and fix him up with a stall for the night. What is it you will be doing in setting up the armory?"

"The main thing is to establish a location to train my troop and a place to store our arms. We also will be recruiting more members. We have to guard against another outbreak like the John Brown affair. It's amazing how unprepared we were for anything like that. I don't know what will happen but we haven't seen the last of the radicals trying to stir up trouble."

"I sure wish there was some way I could be with you."

Tom Jr. could remember that he had a few rough moments when he was sixteen and asked, "Are you having a rough time here?"

"I guess the answer is yes and no. Grandfather Johns and mother are the greatest and Dad is great most of the time. We have trouble over the time I spend studying Greek and Latin and then I do the stupid one like I did today and forget about it being the day for the tutor to be here."

"Dad was drinking pretty heavy today. Is that his usual habit?"

"Not every day. He was under much pressure today to hold himself in while you and Grandpa were here. His natural reaction was to give me a real going over when I appeared. I think there is some reaction between Dad and Grandfather that rubs off on me. For some reason, I discuss anything with Grandpa Johns and he seems to be able to help me. Dad doesn't seem to understand me or want to take time to help me and when he drinks too much as he did today it gets worse, not better. He seemed to get mad at me when Grandpa bought the Spencer rifles and gave me one."

"That Spencer is a great rifle isn't it? I wish I could get enough for the whole company."

"It's a great gun and Grandfather made it even better by honing the trigger or making what he calls a hair trigger. If you want I'll get it and we can set up some targets down here for you to try it."

"We might wake up our Dad and I'm familiar with the gun and with the hair trigger deal. I don't have a hair trigger on mine because it might fire accidentally when we're drilling."

"You do have to be cautious; that's true with any gun. Have you heard anything about the Warrenton Guards down in North Carolina?"

"I have heard Ben Wade was organizing a company. He is my friend and a good man. I think you would be sorely missed here but if you have to make a move before I can take you, Ben would be the best for you."

"Tom, I think we'll have war and soon. I also think it will be over long before I am eighteen. I don't want to sit on the sidelines studying Greek and Latin when I could be doing a man's job. Besides, Dad and I aren't going to get along any better in two years than we do now."

"It's not that bad, is it?"

"I guess you would say it was unpleasant instead of bad."

"Do you want me to talk to Dad at supper?"

"He'll not be down for supper. If he wants anything, Mom or Kitty will take something to him. I don't think you can help the situation. I haven't made up my mind what to do and I haven't talked to grandfather yet. I will before I decide what to do. Enough of my problems; I can't get over how great you look in that gray uniform and what a send-off the yellow sash gives you."

CHAPTER II

Leaving Home

DAN slept fitfully through the night, struggling with what action to take that might solve his problems. He awoke as the animals stirred; not as refreshed as he usually was. As his full consciousness returned, he realized the problem was uppermost in his mind and still had to be solved. If he stayed where he was until he was eighteen, he probably would miss his chance for action and his parents and grandfather would saddle him with running the Daniel Johns affairs. For sure, his grandfather, Daniel Johns, was never going to allow Thomas Wootton to have anything to say about the Johns property or benefit from the operation. After two years, he would be a newcomer to his half brother's troop and might have a time fitting in with established relationships. The only action for a reasonable choice was to go to North Carolina and enlist in the Warrenton Guards, hoping Captain Wade would believe he was eighteen if they had such a restriction. He dressed as quietly and as quickly as he could and went to the slave quarters to get Macon. Kitty was up and ready to leave for her kitchen duties but he had to wake Macon.

"What do you want Master Daniel? Thought you had to stay in today to see Tom off and to talk to your father."

"We'll be back in plenty of time. Come on; there's something that I want to show you," said Dan. He was trying to get Macon away from Kitty without her learning anything about his plans. After they were well away from the slave quarters, he told Macon, "I'm going to Grandfather's house to see what he thinks about joining the Warrenton Guards."

Macon asked, "You going to leave us?"

"If I do, there's a lot I'll miss; especially my mom and my grandfather and Kitty's good cooking and the good times you and I have had hunting and fishing. The trouble is things have a way of changing and I don't like some things here. Maybe Grandfather will see it differently but I think he will agree, though he will not want to see me leave."

"You going to wake up your grandfather this early in the morning?"

"No, Eva comes in each morning and brings him a hot cup of coffee at 4 A.M. He likes to get up early and see that things get started right. There's always some problem to be solved, what I'm doing will fall right in line with what he's doing."

"That Eva sure is a light colored Negro, isn't she?"

"Not only that but she is a pretty woman. She's a mulatto Grandpa inherited from his father-in-law."

"When did your grandmother die?"

"Before I was born. Grandpa tells me my mother looks like my grandmother but from the picture or two I have seen, I don't see the resemblance."

"Wonder why your grandfather never married again. I'm sure that he could find himself a good woman."

"I don't know but Eva takes good care of him and runs his house, maybe he doesn't need a wife. My mother might not like it if he did marry again. We are nearly there now; let me hail grandpa, we don't want to get a load of buckshot to dodge."

Dan stepped behind a tree and whistled three times and got an answering whistle before he went to the door. Eva was there to let him in and Daniel Johns was having his first cup of coffee at his desk.

"Well, this is a pleasant surprise; what brings you two out this early in the morning? I bet you haven't had breakfast because Kitty and Martha usually don't serve for two hours or more."

"That's right Grandpa. We both would like something to eat and I have something I want to discuss with you."

"Eva, take Macon to the kitchen with you and call us when breakfast is ready. Do you want some coffee now, Dan?"

"No thank you. I'll wait until breakfast is ready."

Dan explained the problem he faced with his father and with his wish to get in at the start of the action, if there was going to be trouble. The best solution seemed to be to leave today for North Carolina and the Warrenton Guards. Daniel Johns listened carefully and thought to himself, how your own youth comes back to haunt you in the lives of your grandchildren.

"Dan, you know I'll miss you but I agree you should go and will help you get on your way. You did not bring your rifle, I see, take mine and I will pick up yours when I am over there this morning to say good-by to young Tom and then try to explain to everyone why you had to leave without saying good-by. Eva, send someone out to get Sam. I want him here to measure Dan for a special pair of boots. Let's see; strong boots, a rifle and we will need to fix you up with the tarpaulin and blanket you and I have used often on hunting trips, a knife and one of my pistols, a little money and some food for the trip. Sam can get two horses saddled for you and Macon when he gets your measurements for the boots. Let's go see what Eva and the cook have made for breakfast."

The two Dans finished a breakfast of oatmeal, eggs, bacon and biscuits with plenty of strong coffee. "Macon and I'll not need lunch after a breakfast like this. I guess that he is getting something like this."

Eva replied he's being well fed and Sam was here.

"Send him in. Dan, twist your chair around; Sam needs to get the outline of your two feet. You will have to take off both shoes. Sam, this boy is going into the army in Warrenton and we will have to make him some boots as fast as you can and ship them to him. I want them made with triple soles and well-oiled uppers because he may be walking more than riding. Eva, get that knife and case in my bedroom chest. Sam, I am sending a knife off with Dan and I want you to make a scabbard for it inside the left boot top. A knife hidden in the same place saved my life once and he may find uses for it. No laces on the boots and the tops loose for the trousers to be tucked inside when the weather turns damp and cold. When you are sure of your measurements have my mare saddled and two of the other horses saddled for Dan and Macon. Macon will go and bring back the horses after Dan has been accepted. Eva will see the boys have enough food for the trip and bring more coffee to my desk for Dan and me. Dan come on in when you and Sam are finished."

Dan entered the office saying, "I don't know how I can ever thank you enough for the ease I have in talking to you and the great things you do for me, Grandpa."

"Thank you, Dan. I think we're enough alike that we should be able to understand and help each other, although more years separate us than I like to think about. Here's the new revolver I got for your birthday but you should take it now. I got two of them just as I did for the Spencers. Feel the balance of this gun. This may lead to some great improvements in many kinds of weapons; although I suspect the army brass will be slow to recognize the value. You may need to keep this gun under cover because there is some feeling only officers should carry pistols. If your rifle jams in the middle of a fight, you could save your life because you had another weapon."

"Grandpa you are the greatest ever; you think of everything."

"There are times I wish I did, Dan. You'll be taught many things in the service and will have to learn things they will not teach you. A couple of points may help you. Not everyone in the service is as honest as you are. The fellow next to you may steal just because it is there or he may want to bring you down to his level. Given time, you will know who you can trust. You will make good friends. You also will learn some of your company cannot be trusted to do anything right; they came with two left feet both physically and mentally. The second point is to do whatever you have to do to survive. If you need to fight, use every advantage that you can find. If you need to hide, then hide; if you need to flee, then run as fast as you can to get to where the advantage turns to you. The real winner is the fellow who survives to fight on another day. The generals are interested in who won the battle; what interests you is that you survive."

Eva came in with fresh coffee and announced the horses were at the rack anytime they wanted them and she had the food hamper ready.

Daniel Johns replied, "We'll be out when he has a sip of coffee." The two sat quietly sipping their coffee and savoring their last few minutes together. Johns reached for his grandson, hugged him tightly and said, "Parting will always be hard for us. Let's see, this is Tuesday, April 16; you should make Warrenton by tomorrow night with a stopover at Chase City, more for the horses than for you two young bucks. Tell Macon to come back to me here at the main house. I expect to get a report from him on Friday night. I will go to your parents' house in a few hours and try to explain to them why it has to be this way. You better go now before I try to talk you into staying. Take care."

They parted not knowing the war had already started.

Daniel Johns walked to the door and watched the two ride away, while they were in view. As they disappeared, he sagged, as though he had been hit with a great blow. He struggled back to his desk; motioned to Eva that he wanted more coffee and said, "No one will ever know how hard it was for me to agree and send him on his way. It feels like I tore my viscera out with my own hands. I had planned on bringing him here to live in a few years and showing him how to manage the estate I intended leaving to him with the only provision that his father could not in anyway benefit from the Johns estate. To have tied him to me, now that our state and national affairs are in such a crazy mixed-up mess, would have been wrong. It would be good to have him here but it would destroy his manhood. That would have been worse than seeing him go, not knowing whether we will ever see each other again. If those fools in Charleston have their way and war comes, our whole order could change and managing this estate could be something foreign to what I know. Well, I should go see how the new barns are doing. I need a place to store the salt that will be here next week. Then, to the Wootton household to break the news to them. Eva, I should be back for dinner but do not fix too much; I will not be that hungry."

Dan and Macon rode away from his grandfather's place and took the road to Chase City. As they came to the turn, there was a slight rise and Dan could look back to Daniel Johns' house. He turned his horse and stared without moving or saying anything, as though he was freezing every detail of the place in his mind. After what seemed like a long time to Macon, Dan turned his horse's head and spurred on down the road to Chase City. Dan and Macon rode on in silence, each with his own thoughts as they listened to the plop of the horses' hooves in the soft dirt road and the songs of the birds on a glorious April day. They rode through Green Bay as a few of the natives were starting their day. Dan did not see anyone he recognized for which he was thankful as he did not want to contact anyone who might see the depths of his emotion. He was puzzled at the cross currents flowing through him; he was doing what he should do, yet there were strange tugs at the thought he would not see either his mother or his grandfather on the same basis. He left as a son and as a grandson in a warm easy relationship. He would see them next after some time had passed and after he established an independent life as a soldier. As he rode along puzzling over the feelings, he suddenly remembered his grandfather saying in this life we pay for everything in one fashion or another. He startled Macon by saying: "He is right." And then he had to explain to Macon what had caused the outbreak.

After several hours, they passed through Victoria and through Lunenburg and then they forded the north fork of the Meherrin River. Dan slipped from the saddle and motioned for Macon to let the horses drink from the stream. They let the horses graze on the new grass as they ate a biscuit from the basket that Eva had the cook fill for the trip. They filled their canteens from the river and remounted to continue to Chase City. After several hours' pleasant ride, they forded the south fork of the Meherrin River and after another hour they approached the outskirts of Chase City.

Dan turned to Macon and said: "Let's find a good place to camp for the night. We could go into town and stay with someone I'm sure but I would prefer to stay by ourselves than talk to others tonight. We have plenty of food in the hamper. Come to think about it, I bet there are some good places on the other side of Chase City on the road to Boydton. There must be several creeks running on down to the Roanoke River."

They rode on through Chase City taking the Boydton road to the southeast. About four miles out of town Macon said: "Wait here on the road and let me scout the clump of trees to the west of us. Maybe there is a spring and it would be a good place for our camp."

Macon rode about a quarter of a mile and found a spring there and a grassy plot for their camp. He rode back to the edge of the grove and gave the two-tone whistle which brought Dan in at a gallop. They unsaddled the horses and busied themselves setting up camp. Dan gathered the wood for the fire and started the water for coffee. Macon took the horses to a nearby plot, let them have their roll, took them to the creek for a drink, and tethered them to saplings. He returned to the camp to find Dan spreading his tarpaulin and putting his saddle after it to make a backrest, that way he could stretch out and watch the fire and the sunset. Macon arranged his equipment nearby, both enjoying the last hour of sunshine on a weather-perfect day in April.

Suddenly, Macon sat up, "Listen. There's quail here. I'll make some snares and get us a couple of quail. There's nothing better than roasted quail for breakfast."

Macon looked in the food hamper to see if there was something he could use to make the snares. He picked a towel with a torn edge which gave him a chance to unravel enough thread. It took several minutes of tedious work before he had enough for the snares. Dan followed as Macon searched along the creek bank until he found the locations where he built the snares. He could see there had been quail at the locations by the tracks they had left. Dan had hunted quail often but had always used a gun and a dog.

"Macon, how did you learn to do all this?"

"Master Dan, when you ain't got, you learn to make do."

"Quail have been at these locations but why will they come back to the same place?"

"These are their watering trails and they'll be back here tomorrow morning about daylight. We'll enjoy roasted quail for our breakfast before we leave tomorrow."

Dan said, "Let's get back to our camp. I'm really getting hungry. We should check our horses on the way back to be satisfied they are all right."

Macon said he thought both ideas were good and they turned to the clearing where the horses were tethered.

Dan commented, "I never saw two mares any better matched than these two bays and they want to be together continually. I tried to ride Dolly one day and leave Maude in the pen and you never heard such racket. I had to go back and let Maude out."

"You didn't put a lead rope on Maude?"

"I didn't have to. We were just going to the next field but I think that you could ride Dolly anywhere and Maude would not get more than five feet away. Look at them now; they're grazing almost head to head and if we check later, they'll be laying down side by side."

Dan cut a green twig from one of the willow trees on the way back to the camp. At the camp, he stirred the coffee into the can of hot water and laid the twig across the can. The brew foamed until it touched the twig and dropped back. Macon watched this with as much interest as Dan had watched Macon get the string and set the snares. Dan opened the food hamper and saw the cook had supplied them with fried chicken and baked sweet potatoes. He moved the coffee can to the side of the fire, it would stay hot but not boil; he dipped a cup for Macon and one for himself and said, "Dig in. I bet this will taste good. I don't know what I'll get in the guards but I'm sure it won't be as good as this is. There's something about fried chicken and sweet potatoes that make for a great meal. I haven't looked yet but I expect Eva had the cook put in some chocolate cake. That'll be about perfect with good coffee."

"That Eva has sure been good to you and to your grandfather."

"She's a nicer person than many white people I know and I think she knows Grandpa intended I come live with him in a few years and take over the operation of the place. Grandpa seems to have a knack for running the farms. I'm not sure I could ever learn. He seems to sense what problems may develop and when the time is right to act. I don't think I could ever do that. When I think I see a problem, I jump into action, though I recognize Grandpa's way is a lot better. I think everyone knows he is fair and does act after thinking the thing through. That may be the reason he seems to have no trouble on his places when some of his neighbors have something going continually."

"Is this a good time for you to tell me about belonging to Mr. Johns and working for the Woottons?"

"Could not be a better time. Do you want some more coffee? Let's see if I'm right in guessing Eva had some chocolate cake put in here for us. Yes, here it is. Good old Eva, she wouldn't let me down. I guess you know my father is thirteen years older than my mother. That did not make any difference to my mother but it's one of the things that irritates my grandfather. My mother was only fifteen when they married and Grandpa thought she was too young to marry. She should not marry an old man who had been married once before and had a nine-year-old son. Then, though they seem to be happily married, it turns out my father has a way of dreaming big dreams but they do not have any practical application. He knows the classics, is generous to a fault, has never been able to manage his money, can be charming and witty, trusts people he should not trust and cannot understand why they let him down, and sometimes drinks too much, so far as Daniel Johns is concerned. I have heard that no father ever thinks his son-in-law is good enough for his daughter and Grandpa thinks he has proof. Daniel Johns wants his daughter to have the life he has worked hard to make for her but he is bound and determined that her husband isn't going to get a chance to spend the Johns money. He has shown me his will and he covers the point several times and he has executed and recorded a document called a deed of loan which covers the 500 acres where we live, the seven slaves for the place and the horse my mother uses. All this with the provision my father can in no way control any of the property and the loan can be revoked. Both men may wish they could do some things as the other one can but they're never going to let anyone know they feel that way. I would not say they hate each other but they don't often agree and it's not going to get any better. That is the reason you belong to Daniel Johns but work at the Wootton's. I think I'm about ready to turn in; how about you?" He did not get an answer and turned to see what had happened and found Macon was sound asleep. Dan rolled up in his blanket and was soon sleeping much better than he had the night before.

The next thing Dan heard was the crackle of the fire as the flames reached to kiss the new wood. As he rolled over, he saw that Macon was threading two quail onto a green stick and preparing to cook them when the fire reduced to more coal than flame. "Good morning, Macon. I guess I really slept last night. I didn't hear you get up and I see you caught the quail as you said you would. That is great. I'm glad I saw how you did that."

"We could have had more but I didn't think we needed more

than one apiece. I'll go check Maude and Dolly if you will watch this and give it a turn now and then."

Dan got the coffee can on the fire and spooned in the coffee and got a twig to keep it from boiling over. He turned the birds as they browned and the smell got better the closer they came to being done. Macon came back with Maude and Dolly and took them down to the creek for a drink. When he got back and had them saddled, Dan had the birds and the coffee ready and said, "Come on, let's eat."

It didn't take long for the two hungry boys to put away the breakfast. Dan licked his fingers and took a last swig of coffee. "There's something about cooking and eating around a campfire in a pretty place you cannot really describe to someone who has never experienced it. Whatever you have, tastes a little bit better than if it's eaten at any other place. I hate to leave this pretty place but we have to get on the road if we want to get to Warrenton this afternoon. We have to cross the Roanoke River this morning and shortly after we'll be in North Carolina. Let's fill our canteens with this good spring water and be on our way."

They swung aboard the horses and before noon had crossed the Roanoke and were on the road to Norlina. "We must be in North Carolina now, Macon. Let's stop at the first farmhouse that is close to the road and see if we can get a stretch and a bite to eat before we head on down to Warrenton. I'm sure that we can make out on what we have in the hamper but I feel like a hot meal at a table would be good. These people may have some news about Captain Wade."

A mile on down the road, there was a neat looking farmhouse and they turned in and were received warmly. The farmer had heard a company was being formed at Warrenton but did not know any of the details. The two were soon back on the road, passed through Norlina and reached Warrenton by mid-afternoon. Dan asked where he could find Captain Wade. He was directed to the law office of Peter Spruill who informed him Captain Wade was in Garysburg but would be back on the night train. When Dan stated why he wanted to see Captain Wade, Peter said he was a sergeant in Captain Wade's company and Dan would be welcome to stay with him. They would see Captain Wade in the morning.

CHAPTER III

Homefront, 1861

*E*VA watched as Daniel Johns returned from the Wootton household. She thought he looked like he had aged twenty years since this morning. She turned back into the house and went to the kitchen; poured a cup of coffee for Daniel and gave it a good shot of brandy. When Daniel got to his office, she was there with the steaming hot coffee.

"Eva, you always know what I need. I had a rough time with those people this morning. Even Kitty was yowling she had lost her son, Macon. I think I put most of their tears to rest but none of them liked what I've done. They now at least accept that it's done and they should make the best of what they have left. People usually get to this end point but sometimes with a lot more torment than they exhibited. This may be because they are smarter than most or that they realize they live as they do because of my patience in their use of my property. Anyhow, I have that session behind me and I'll never know if I was right in helping the young buck do what he wanted to do. Let's hope some sense will prevail in this land. I would like to believe it will but reason tells me we're a bunch of stubborn idiots rushing pell-mell into a great disaster. I guess there is nothing I will or can do that will change what Yancy and those fools do. I should learn to live with those things I cannot change. Eva, with another cup of good coffee with that black cream, I think I can eat a little dinner."

"Mr. Johns, the cook has a chicken-fried steak and mashed potatoes ready for you. That and a little country gravy should make you feel better."

"I'm sure it will. Tell Sam to have my runabout ready as I have to go into Green Bay this afternoon. I had forgotten that if we have trouble, coffee will be scarce and I should pick up a few sacks of green coffee beans. I think they will keep if we can find a good place for them. I'll be back for supper. Make a list if there is anything you want me to get in Green Bay. I'll wait for the afternoon train from Richmond and bring the mail and the papers back."

"We need baking soda and bluing and there may be other things. I think we could use more kerosene but I'll check the supply and make the list."

Daniel thought over the early morning visit with young Dan and the emotions that parting with his grandson stirred in his own soul. Parts of the experience were as warm as other parts were painful. I guess we humans always have to pay for our pleasures, he mused, but sometimes it seems we pay more than we get in return. Maybe, we need to plan better but how can we plan for the effect of those things that seem to be unrelated to our lives and yet have a major effect on our emotions and sometimes on our lives. Oh well, we have to live this afternoon and not worry about what happened this morning. God, how I disliked the emotional turmoil that went on this morning at the Wootton household. As much as I dislike Thomas Ballard Wootton, I have to give the devil his due; he was a better balance wheel for those two females than I thought he would be. He may lose his control later or it may be his military training gives him the emotional rules to follow. He still is not going to get any of the Johns' money to spend but he may have something in his makeup I had not seen before. It hadn't occurred to me but maybe the way I pay for having such a great daughter is by having such a no-good son-in-law.

Daniel aroused himself from this introspection, got the shopping list from Eva and started for Green Bay. When he got to the little village, he found the town was discussing the bombardment of Fort Sumter and most of them rejoicing that the Federals were being taught a lesson. Daniel went to the railroad office and confirmed with the telegraph operator the attack had begun last Friday, April 12 and the fort had surrendered on Monday. He promised to get Daniel a copy of the *Richmond Daili Despatch* when the afternoon train came through. Daniel hurried about town to get his shopping finished and was amazed that everyone was elated at the bombardment of Fort Sumter. He was puzzled until he realized they didn't think of it as the start of war but as an end to the crisis that had been brewing for months. People cannot live with the tension the fort made for the South; they're happy the crisis is gone and the tension is relieved. Though the action is stupid, it seems it's good because it ended the crisis. Daniel thought I wish with all my being it might be an ending and then I could celebrate with them. It is, I believe, the start of a civil war that may destroy all that we now hold dear. This gives Lincoln power he could never have gotten otherwise, and leaves us with limited means and a leader in Jefferson Davis who many of us believe is not capable of getting the job done, even if we had the means. Daniel finished his shopping and got back to the railroad station before the afternoon train arrived from Richmond.

Nearly everyone in the little town was at the station when the train arrived. There was a festive mood in the gathering and the arrival of the train seemed to be the cause of great shouts and waving of hats by the crowd at the station and the passengers and the train crew. Daniel mused, I hope they'll have as much enthusiasm for the chores and the sacrifices they'll shortly be called upon to make.

Someone asked Daniel if he was happy and Daniel replied he was never happy to see anyone hurt or killed.

In their minds, old man Johns was getting too old to understand the great victory the South had completed. Daniel got his copy of the Richmond paper and returned to his house without stopping at his daughter's place. He told Eva he could not take two emotional sessions at the Wootton household in one day and they would do just as well by getting the copy of the paper the next morning.

Daniel attended to the estate chores the next morning and postponed going to the Wootton household until after dinner. He mused that I am no better than a kid; I postpone facing unpleasant tasks hoping they'll go away or somehow events will preclude my having to do the things I find unpleasant to do. He told Eva he would stop by the Wootton place on the way to Green Bay and then return to Wootton's for supper. That way we can digest the papers for two days and it is always better to have discussions around a meal. The emotions seem to be more controllable when there's a meal in progress; I wonder if that is the basis for the Irish wake? Could be. They are so sad when they are sad that they need something to bolster their being or they would not survive. My wife, God rest her soul, could be so depressed I would fear for her life but a good meal seemed to lift her enough to make it to the next crisis. Could be the result of the mistreatment the race had for so many years when they starved. I must find the dogwood spoon I carved when we first started courting and see that Martha gets it. I was too poor to have a silver spoon made for her but I wanted to show her it was spooning I was interested in and I had hopes for a better life. She got to enjoy the better life with me but always worried it would not last. I sure miss her but in a way it's better she did not live to see our daughter throw her life away on that no-good old man she married.

Daniel dropped the Richmond paper at the Wootton's and made arrangements to have supper with them on his way back. He found the town was still showing enthusiasm for clearing the fort from Charleston harbor, almost as though it was something they had done. Everyone was repeating Jefferson Davis' phrase that all that they wanted was to be left alone. Daniel thought any day you fire on the flag and confiscate government property and expect you will be left alone is expecting something unlikely to happen. He got his paper when the train arrived from Richmond and made arrangements with the station master to get him a paper every day. He thought he would be in town about every other day or he would send someone in to get the mail and the papers.

This pattern of meeting the afternoon train and supper at the Wootton's developed in the next few weeks and supplied the best communication Daniel and his son-in-law had ever had. It didn't change Daniel's opinion about the man; he was a spendthrift and no good but they had more common ground for discussion than ever before. Between the two of them, they knew many players who were striding across the stage and could expand on the events as reported by the press. They were elated when Macon returned and reported young Dan had arrived in Warrenton and made contact with Peter Spruill. Tom and Martha knew the Spruill boy's mother and father and could remember Peter as a young lad. They were delighted with the further report on the camp that had been developed as Macon returned from delivering the boots.

They were surprised at the pace the new government got things done. The national loan was over-subscribed by sixty percent and within two months the post office was ready to function. The new state department was a going institution before Sumter was fired on. Daniel and Tom were amused they lost no time in finding a berth for Yancy that took him out of the country. They knew Davis' fine hand was involved in the move as he did not want a hot head like Yancy around when he had a tough administration job to get organized. Yancy would be bound to cause embarrassment and maybe downright trouble if left around. They predicted a way would be found to keep him busy in some other part of the world. Later on they found he was the ambassador to Turkey. Daniel and Tom had to chuckle at that two-edged appointment.

They heard from Ethel that young Dan had looked her up as his company passed through Richmond and later received Dan's letter from Norfolk. The papers were full of the Baltimore riots and the Virginia takeover of the arsenal at Harpers Ferry before they seceded from the union. Then they learned the Federals had abandoned and tried to destroy the Norfolk base.

With the letter from Dan confirming he was at Norfolk, Tom said, "You can count on the Woottons being in the thick of things. Tom Jr. has to be part of the unit that has taken over Harpers Ferry and Dan is protecting what the Federals gave us without a fight at Norfolk." Strange as it is, he thought, Harpers Ferry cannot be adequately defended against any determined opponent. We have to chase the Federals out of there and the Norfolk base could be held and supplied and they give it to us. Tom Sr. was pleased that good use was made of the equipment at both locations. The machinery was moved from Harpers Ferry to Richmond and the armaments at Norfolk supplied many needs through the South.

They were amazed the Confederate Congress voted on May 21 to move the capitol to Richmond when the electorate in Virginia did not vote on seceding until May 23. Daniel and Tom discussed this move at some length; Tom thought that it was a disastrous move from his military background. Daniel agreed. From a military point of view, it was the worst possible decision. Several papers commented in vain. Such a move probably would cause the new administration to focus their attention on defending Richmond when the really important issues were in other locations. A capitol at Atlanta or Raleigh would have better transportation facilities and many other things that would make them a better choice than Richmond. To increase the hazards, the armament facilities captured at Harpers Ferry were moved to Richmond. By any stretch of the imagination, these should have been placed in Atlanta.

Daniel explained, "As much as I agree with you, Tom, on the foolishness of the move to Richmond, there is a political side to the problem that apparently took precedent, though I don't think it should have. First, Montgomery is a dull dry little town and the politicians always like a little refreshment and amusement. That state legislature is considering the passage of a law banning the use of grain to make any alcohol products because the grains should be used in the war effort. No politician thinks he can get his job done without a good stiff drink. How would you get a consensus without a little libation to help get your point across is what a politician would say. They must be more than a little afraid the state may shut down the manufacture of alcohol. And about entertainment, I'm sure there is no female in Montgomery that's flipping her skirts around; if she did, she would be shunned or run out of town. The same things can be said for Raleigh and North Carolina may shut down the manufacture of alcohol. Raleigh's not quite as straight-laced as Montgomery but compared to Richmond's night life, it would be a distant second."

Martha interrupted. "I don't believe Mr. Davis had anything like that in mind. I think he is a statesman and would not countenance a move because there were more bars and night life in Richmond."

Daniel added, "I would agree generally. However, Mr. Davis faces some practical problems and to get what he wants in one area he may find he has to give in others. He can be a stubborn old devil and usually is. If the move was proposed for its real reason, he might bow his neck and refuse. If proposed because there are better hotels in Richmond, he probably would agree, although he really knew about other considerations. He now has and will continue to have problems with three concepts."

Tom said, "I think you are right. Martha, I don't think you have heard your father outline three other points that make problems for Mr. Davis."

Daniel said, "Tom and I agreed the other day that Davis has three concepts, ideas or problems that could make for our downfall. The first might be called Davis, the man; the second would be states' rights and the third would be the difference between legal right and revolution.

"First Davis, the man. He knows that he has the best military mind available. Your husband and I wouldn't agree with him but even if we're wrong in our judgment of the man, his job will make him focus his attention on other things. He probably will make some serious errors and he's so constituted he cannot even countenance the thought that anything he has done could have been done any better by any other mortal. He isn't in good health and only has one eye. The work load he now has is more than he can adequately cover and will increase. I don't have the first-hand knowledge Tom has of his sad history in choosing men for key positions but I think it's true and will be a millstone around our necks on some future date.

"The second concept, states' rights, will be troublesome in that the states think they are independent of the central government. There are some signs we have problems with this now and the problems will multiply. The states seceded because their central government was making decisions they did not agree were right or logical. When their new central government makes decisions the state governor doesn't like, there'll be problems. You already can see this showing up in the problem of who gets to appoint a general.

"The third concept is even more weird and difficult to believe that Davis and his friends really believe it themselves. This has to do with the idea they haven't started a revolution; what they have done is very legal and within their rights. Whatever the merits of the constitutional question about a state's right to secede went by the board when they fired on the flag and took federal property. Davis must be playing games with himself when he mouths the words that all we want is to be left alone. Somehow this weird idea has to play a part in the move to Richmond. If the Federals will leave us alone, Richmond is a more pleasant place to live than is Montgomery. I don't know anyone who thinks that Lincoln will buy the leave-us-alone thesis. Lincoln doesn't have resources to do anything at the moment and neither do we but the longer we hang on this falsehood, the more trouble we can expect. We need to focus on the fact we have started a civil war and we need to gird our flanks to see if we can be successful.

"That's an awful long answer but I can't seem to boil it down."

Martha asked, "Do you think we will lose?"

"I hope not," replied Daniel, "but we'll have to be lucky to win. When we start knowing some things for sure that just aren't true, the outlook isn't hopeful. How do you see it, Tom?"

"Hard to judge. We have some strong points and so do they. If the struggle is over in a short time, we win. If it goes on for years, watch out."

The three eagerly scanned the June papers which carried the account of Davis' move to Richmond. He was ill and got little rest on the train trip as every little town thought they had to see their new president and to hear a few words from him. He was on the ragged edge when he got to Richmond. Only his strong sense of duty carried him through the ceremonies he had to endure as he arrived in the new capitol.

There was much pride by the people in Virginia and by the residents of Richmond that they had been awarded the prize of the Confederate capitol. The few editors who indicated it might be less than the most desirable thing to do were discounted because they wanted the capitol in their area. Tom thought it was a major strategic miss but no one in the Confederate service would dare to risk his assignment on any comment the President made anything other than great decisions. If any of the Federal generals thought about it, they did not want to show what an advantage the rebels had given them for fear it might be changed.

During June and on into July, they watched as the Federals assured that Maryland stayed in the union. While maybe no one would agree the way they went about it was legal, Tom had to agree the result was needed to protect and to support Washington. The Federals did not have a logical choice in trying to choose a new capitol. Any change would have been humiliating and probably would have fractured the Federal cause.

McClellan's advance from Ohio to open rail communication with Washington and the Eastern seaboard made possible the new state of West Virginia in June. Tom could see General Scott's planning in this and it made much strategic sense. They did the same thing they did in Maryland with less fuss and feathers and gave the government in Richmond a real black eye. Since the secession movement was largely an emotional knee-jerk, Tom and Daniel had a hard time trying to decide which was the greater value to the Federals; the securing of the B & O railroad or the secession of West Virginia from Virginia. The battle at Philippi was not much as a military exercise but with the Confederates fleeing without their pants and their armaments was a major propaganda victory. It damaged the idea that one Confederate. could whip any three Yankees.

The *Richmond Despatch* for Tuesday, July 23, gave Daniel and Tom their first news of the long awaited battle near Manassas. Everyone had been reading about the preparations and Tom added he hoped Lincoln did not subscribe to the Richmond papers. Those damn fools blabbed about every troop that came through town. On the other hand, he hoped someone was subscribing to the Washington and New York papers as these nuts were supplying the best intelligence that could be had about what the Federals were doing.

The news was a bigger boon to the southern spirits than the news from the Big Bethel skirmish the month before. The headlines, this time, said that it was a brilliant victory, that 1,000 to 1,500 Federal troops were killed, and applauded the heroic conduct of our troops. Tom's evaluation was the long-awaited battle had gone our way this time and we may have been more lucky than good. If we had really won the day, we would have pressed the Federals as they retreated to Washington. The time to strike with everything you have is when the enemy is demoralized and in retreat. He assumed we didn't follow up on the apparent "great" victory because we could not. In a few days they heard young Tom had been in the fight and came through it without injury, although he had some casualties in his company. They also got the report the Federals had been engaging in some long-range shelling of the Confederate batteries at Sewell's point but young Dan and his troop who were guarding the battery did not suffer any casualties. The news their two sons were in the operations but were safe brought great joy and thanks to both households. This was heightened even more with the news that young Tom was now a captain.

They began to detect strange crosscurrents in the affairs of the Confederacy. There were stories some governors had stopped accepting volunteers because they were not needed and there was no need to incur the expense. Daniel and Tom wished this might be true but it appeared Jeff Davis was going to have more than one battle to fight and the worst ones might be those he had to fight with people who were supposed to be his friends. The following months brought more examples of bitter exchanges between the various state governors and the central government. Most of the states viewed their position on many matters as being their rights and not subject to review or concurrence by the central government. Anyway, this was one of the real reasons for withdrawing from the union. Poor old Jeff, thought Tom; he'll wish he had the simple task of a military command instead of trying to produce a reason the states should pay at least some attention to the central government.

Tom thought the stories about the terrible things that the Federals were doing to the civilian population were prime examples of bad reporting. They were slanted to show the Federals were brutes and the southern armies contained only gentlemen who would never stoop to do such dastardly things. Anyone, thought Tom, should know there is no way you can move an army through the countryside without leaving marks that it has passed. If a battle ensues, there has to be destruction of personal property and loss of civilian life. There are as many thugs in the North as there are in the South. After an army has marched for a day, the soldiers will do whatever is convenient to sustain themselves. Maybe, thought Tom, the editors feel there is a need to arouse the public.

Daniel thought part of the problem stemmed from the concept the states had adopted as they withdrew. While everyone admitted to himself most of the reason for the withdrawal was a knee-jerk emotional action, there was the concept the states had a right to secede and form a new union. From this, Davis drew his famous line "that all we want is to be left alone." That wish was never possible. When the states took Federal property by force and Davis acquiesced to the demand that something be done about Sumter, those acts changed the secession into a revolt without any doubt. Maybe one of the reasons there was no follow-up to the victory at Manassas was if they return to their territory, we will not molest them. Tom thought war was war and the South should gird itself for a long and bitter struggle. The South had a chance to deal the Federals a severe blow by following up on the victory. Maybe the South did not because they did not have the ability or because of the all-we-want-is-to-be-left-alone philosophy. Whatever the reason, we now have lost the time to strike and we are in for a tough time if we allow the Federals to withdraw and re-group and then test us at another time and location. Daniel's reaction was he thought Tom was right as rain; Davis and many southern leaders were hung up with the concept the Federals weren't fair in war actions they took. The people of Charleston were enraged when they saw the blockade ships on station outside their harbor; for them it was totally unfair for the Federals to do that. They had no right to do such a thing. The Federals' refusal to send slaves back across the lines was viewed as gross disregard of the laws of the Federal government. It just was not fair. Tom thought everyone in the South should change their ideas that this might be a genteel aberration; or that life would soon continue in its smooth and uninterrupted manner. Daniel thought I don't think people will quit dreaming until the great hand of fate grabs them by the neck and jerks them upright. And from what he could see near the end of the year, it looked like the big hand would start setting people upright in 1862.

CHAPTER IV

Enlistment

DAN heard the cook stoking the fires downstairs. He had to think for a minute to decide where he was and then the rush of the last few days put the spur to him. He had to get food for Macon and get him started back to Green Bay. He dressed hurriedly and asked the cook to fix something for Macon as he went to the barn to see if Macon was awake and was getting packed to return. Macon was up and dressed and had started to curry Maude and Dolly. Dan told him to bring both horses to the hitching rail when he had them saddled and he would bring the food out to him. Dan brought out a tray and said, "I had the cook make us egg and bacon sandwiches. The coffee sure smells good. We have been together ever since I can remember and I'll miss seeing you every day as I shall miss being home and seeing my parents and grandfather, but it seems things like this happen to us and there is little or nothing we can do about it. The cook will bring out the hamper when she gets it filled for your return trip. I think you know Maude will lead a little better than Dolly. Be sure you report back to Daniel Johns; he may want you to stay at the main house instead of going back to my parents now that I have left home. Lord knows when we'll see each other, again but we'll have to be together. I think this will be a short war if war does begin, but my father and others think it'll last a long time. Whatever does happen, we'll find some way to see each other again. Good-bye Macon. Take care on your way home. Tell Grandpa that I'm fine."

The cook brought out the food hamper. Macon tied it on the saddle and mounted Dolly as he picked up Maude's lead rope. As he turned the corner, he looked back, waved and gave the two-tone whistle they had used to train the new dog. Dan waved, returned the whistle and took the coffee pot and cups back to the cook.

The cook said, "Mr. Spruill will be down shortly and I have some hot coffee if you want to sit at the dining table."

Dan sat at the table savoring the hot coffee and before he finished, Peter Spruill sat down for his breakfast. Dan told him he had his breakfast with Macon as he started him back to Green Bay, Virginia. Peter said his office was next door to Captain Wade's drugstore and they could check to see if the captain was in and if not, Dan could wait in the law office. As they got near the drugstore, they saw several people were crowded around someone seated on the bench reading from a newspaper. Peter told Dan it was Captain Wade who was reading and as they got to the group, Wade looked up and asked Peter to take over the reading. He explained, "We may as well use our lawyer's talents to read and answer any questions." Peter saw it was a copy of the *Richmond Despatch* for April 16 that Wade must have brought back from Garysburg last night. He began to read an article titled, THE BOMBARDMENT OF FORT SUMTER. Dan was amazed to learn the war had started last Friday. The fort withstood two days' bombardment without loss of life and Major Anderson had left under the Stars and Stripes with the band playing Yankee Doodle. Major Anderson and his men were being taken north by ship and Major Ripley and his two hundred men had taken possession of Fort Sumter by order of General Beauregard.

There was several seconds silence as Peter finished reading the article, each person testing in his own mind just what the start of a shooting war might mean to him. Captain Wade broke the silence to say he learned at Garysburg that Lincoln had wired Governor Ellis to supply troops to suppress the rebellion in South Carolina and the governor had not only refused to have anything to do with firing on a sister state but had ordered Fort Caswell and other installations be secured for the state of North Carolina.

Captain Wade turned to Peter and others to say he had brought back the tents they needed. He thought they should set the tents up in the fairgrounds and get the men sworn-in that afternoon. The sooner we get everyone together, the sooner we can begin training in earnest. Peter introduced Dan saying here was a fellow from Virginia with a new Spencer rifle who wanted to join us.

"I'm sure we want you to join us if you know how to use the Spencer," said Wade. "Peter, those tents are on the wagon at my house if you will detail someone to harness my team and get them down to the fairgrounds, while you and I work out what we'll need for the swearing-in ceremony."

Peter looked around and said, "Dan, this is Will Skinner who is one of us. Can you help Will get the team and the load down to the fairgrounds? Wade and I'll join you there when we finish the draft and we'll get the rest of the company down there before nightfall. I'll bring some food down for the four of us. We should be there by noon or shortly after that."

Will led the way to Captain Wade's barn and they soon had the load headed for the fairgrounds. Will said they had about five miles to go and Dan thought to himself five miles was about as far as this scrawny team could take the load. They were no match for the big well-fed animals he used at the Johns place. They traveled west through the edge of the town and Dan thought Warrenton is no different from little towns in Virginia. For some reason, he thought there should be something to signify this was North Carolina, instead here it was, a little bit smaller than Farmville and a little bit larger than Green Bay.

They pulled into the fairgrounds which turned out to be about a twenty-acre level piece of ground with a few shade trees and a pretty brook along its western edge. Dan thought I bet that Captain Wade will have us establish camp near the west boundary to be near the water and to leave the rest of the area open for drill. He suggested to Will they pull on through the grounds and wait in the shade for the Captain. Will stretched out on the load when they stopped and was soon asleep as far as Dan could tell. Dan walked to the brook and discovered the brook started at a spring just north of the property and made a wide turn as it left the south end of the fairgrounds. As the brook made the turn east, it had developed a pool that contained a few sun perch and would have made a good place to swim except Dan found the water was cold. That has to be a year-round spring thought Dan or the water would not be so cold.

Dan got back to the wagon as Captain Wade and Peter rode into the fairground followed by four blacks in a wagon. Dan woke Will who yawned and slid down from the load of tents.

Captain Wade smiled, "Couldn't sleep, Will, I see. You boys have spotted the location where we want to lay out our camp. Peter, you walk out about a hundred yards and you and I'll sight Will and Dan as they drive stakes for tent locations. We want a tent every twenty feet and after we get ten tents in this row, we will move south twenty feet and put in another row. We'll only need three rows now but will add others as we need them. After we get the locations spotted, Will will drive the wagon by each location and we'll take off a tent. Peter, have your blacks use those axes to cut some more tent stakes in the woods over there and we'll soon have our company camp started."

The group busied themselves with their tasks, and soon there was the outline of the camp. Wade noticed how Dan went about the work and saw this wasn't the first time Dan had established camp. When he saw Dan take a shovel and put a drainage berm around the first tent, he called the rest of the group to show them that he wanted berms around all the tents. They broke for lunch when Wade's cook arrived with a big hamper of food and finished the rest of the thirty tents in the afternoon. Wade spotted the location for the three headquarters tents which made a triangle north of the first row.

Captain Wade looked over their work and told the group that was enough for the first day. "We can all go home now and tomorrow we'll want some more people out here to fix a cook area and to dig a latrine trench and then we'll come back Sunday night after supper and spend the night here; we'll be ready for training to begin on Monday morning. There should be fifty men here to start with and we'll have more before the month is finished. Peter, let's see if we can get the people together tonight after supper in front of the court house. We'll have our swearing-in ceremony and let everyone know when they should be here at the camp. Some may have problems or questions we can help them with between now and Monday morning's training schedule."

They returned to town and Dan and Peter washed for supper and afterwards made the rounds spreading the word about the meeting. The crowd gathered by the court house, some because they were part of the company being formed, some because they thought they might be interested in joining, and some because they did not have anything else to do and thought they might find out what was happening. Captain Wade appeared with a portly gentleman in tow and someone in the group told Dan this was the local Baptist minister. Dan thought he looked like the type of fellow his grandfather would describe as having put away more chicken and gravy than any two people should have done. Captain Wade made a short speech telling the crowd what had happened at Charleston and explaining this company was being formed for a year's service to protect and defend the state of North Carolina. He asked those present who would join with him to step forward and be sworn in. Dan thought the setting and the oath made an impressive beginning for the company. Following the oath, Captain Wade asked the minister to close the meeting with a blessing. The old windbag delivered a long prayer; people began to shift their weight and sigh but the minister would not be deterred. Dan though he started with Gabriel and covered every detail on the way to tonight's activity. Dan made a note to see if there was not another church available for Sunday services. If the old windbag had someone to say a few amens along the way, he would continue for two hours.

Saturday morning Peter and Dan met Captain Wade at the fairgrounds and with the blacks from the Wade and Spruill households, the group finished setting up the tents, the cooking and serving area, and dug the latrine trench. Dan rigged a large tarpaulin between the trees to make a shelter for part of the cooking area and to cover the serving area. Will showed up later in the day with Wade's wagon and team and made three round trips, bringing in cooking pots and supplies. As they ended the day, they thought they had everything they would need to start camp on Monday morning, including a large load of wood brought in by Will and the blacks.

Dan suggested on the way back to town that he bring his gear back out after supper and stay at the camp as a precaution against anything going wrong before the group got there on Sunday night. Wade thought the suggestion was a capital idea and Peter said he would have the cook bring Dan his meals. Dan thanked them and replied that would be good but if it was too much bother, he could make do on his own. Peter insisted it would be his pleasure and he probably would bring dinner out himself and spend the afternoon with Dan. Dan thought to himself he had dodged the issue of listening to the old windbag and would have a pleasant day in camp. There was a chance of a shower before morning but with a good tent and his tarpaulin and bedroll, he would be dry and comfortable and would have a pleasant feeling of accomplishment instead of sitting through a boring sermon on hellfire and damnation.

Sunday morning, the cook appeared with Dan's breakfast and an umbrella Peter had sent for Dan. The rain really was not that bad; it was a light mist with occasional brief showers. Dan had a fire going when the cook arrived and was soon comfortable with a pot of hot coffee, fresh homemade rolls, jam and bacon. Dan thought I never expected the army to feed this well and come to think of it, maybe this isn't army food. I bet we find days when this type of treatment will be remembered as a pleasant dream.

The cook looked over the layout for the cooking area and thought it is camping out for sure but adequate. "Mr. Peter said that either the Wade's cook or me would be the cook for the company. If I gets the call, there is enough here to get started. I hope they are counting on two or three more people to help with the preparation, serving and the clean up. If they expect to serve meat, we should have a fire pit and a grate of some kind or a spit and a couple of pitch forks to help turn the meat. I'll talk to Mr. Peter when he gets back from church."

Peter showed up about one. They had a pleasant meal, a chance to visit and time to explore the area. Peter sent the cook back to the house to bring supper and to bring Peter's bedroll. The rest of the company drifted in during the evening with Captain Wade showing up near bedtime. Peter had told his cook he should return at daylight and to bring another black with him and the Captain would have two of his blacks sent over in the morning. The cook was told to get ready for breakfast and then to use the iron triangle to wake everyone for breakfast and the day's training.

Training began by squads with Dan being assigned to Peter's squad. Dan enjoyed the rhythm of the march and the commands as the squad learned how to respond as a unit instead as individuals. By the end of the day, they had learned from Peter, their sergeant, how to execute all the squad commands. Captain Wade seemed pleased and announced they would have a brief squad review tomorrow morning and then start drilling as a company.

Day rushed upon day as they practiced their new art of marching, turning out for guard duty, target practice, and trying to crawl through the underbrush to surprise the enemy. The town blacksmith made bayonets for their rifles. Their company had a hodgepodge of rifles and the best some could do was to carry a shotgun.

Captain Wade thought they would be able to get rifles for every-one when they got to the regimental camp at Garysburg. On April 29, one week after they had started their training, the group gained another thirty-five enlistments.

Captain Wade had Sergeant Peter Spruill take his squad to the field and demonstrate their knowledge of the manual of arms and squad commands. Dan and the rest of the squad were proud of their precision and the sharpness with which they executed their orders. Captain Wade had the new recruits divided into squads and started their training. The new recruits made all the mistakes that new recruits make, turning the wrong way, starting on the wrong foot, etc. Dan and the "old-timers" thought it was the funniest show they had ever seen. No one reminded them that they were doing the same silly things just a week before.

On Saturday, May 3, Macon arrived with his new boots, a bundle of clothing, a box of Kitty's cookies, a note from his parents and one from his grandfather.

Reading these notes brought a rush of tender memories of his home and the people he had left.

His grandfather's note read, "Dear Dan: The news that you were gone was quite a shock to the Wootton household but your father and I were able to convince your mother and Kitty that you had grown up faster than they had observed. I don't know that they like me any better for helping you but at least they see that maybe time got away from them. We meet most every day and compare notes on the current events. You have our hopes for the best for you and for your safe return. Love, Grandpa."

Next Dan turned to his mother's note; it read, "Dan dearest: You can not imagine the shock I had when Grandpa told us you had gone to Warrenton. I thought my heart would stop and never start again. I think Kitty cried as much as I did. We both thought we had lost our sons. Little by little, your father and grandfather made us see that we were holding on to ideas of you as our baby boys and now suddenly you were men. I don't know that I like it but I'm beginning to accept it. God keep you safe and you know that we love you. Mother."

He got paper from Peter's office and wrote a note to his parents and to Daniel Johns. He wrote to his parents "Dear Mom and Dad: Thank you for your letter. I, too, had pangs as I left. You'll never know how hard it was to turn and ride on after pausing for a last look. As grandpa says, 'We pay for everything we get in this world' and it seemed true as I left.

"I am learning a lot of new things and we have a good company. Sergeant Spruill is a great friend and a fine person.

"Write to me at Garysburg. We should be going there soon. My love and a hug to everyone. Dan"

He wrote to Daniel Johns, "Dear Grandpa, You should see some of the guns we have in our company. Some of them could have seen service in the revolutionary war. Everyone agrees that my Spencer rifle is great. Some of the boys brought shotguns and one poor fellow trains with a crooked stick. He tells me he has killed as many Yankees with it so far as I have with my fancy rifle. He could be right. He always sees the funny side of things. They think everyone will get rifles when we get to Garysburg. Love, Dan."

He gave the letters to Macon and got his food for the return trip. As Macon was ready to turn the corner, there was the two-tone whistle from Macon and a reply by Dan as a salute for the good times they have had together and the hope there will be more.

The company continued to get a few more men and began to feel they knew how to work as a unit. Each squad of eight men developed a special relationship that made each member watch out for the other person. They were turned into a fury of activity by the news they would move to Garysburg on Wednesday, May 15. All gear, including tents, had to be packed and loaded onto the cars. Dan thought when we do this a few more times we will have a better system than we have this time. Anyway, they got packed and loaded and the train picked them up Wednesday morning and delivered them to Garysburg in mid-afternoon. They hurried to get the cooking area established because they were starved; no one had thought to provide for food, while they were in route. While the cook was fixing their meal, the rest got the company's allotted space laid out and the tents erected.

In Warrenton they had been known as the Warrenton Guards and at Garysburg they were known as Captain Benjamin O. Wade's company as they were mustered into the Confederate States service on Saturday, May 18. Shortly after, they were renamed Company A of the 2nd Regiment, North Carolina Volunteers. This was shortly changed to Company F of the 2nd Regiment and Dan did not know why the changes were made but there was much confusion on many things with the clerks at regimental headquarters. North Carolina had an agreement that they would permit their troops to serve in the Confederate armies with the Confederate government paying the troops but the state would furnish the uniforms. They barely got their issue of N.C. uniforms and their first pay ($11 U.S.) when they were ordered to Richmond on Wednesday, May 22.

The company was full of rumors about where they were going and for most of the company, Richmond was a new and exciting experience. Dan got permission to visit his Aunt Ethel who promptly put Dan into a robe until her seamstress could get his N.C. uniform altered to fit him. She was amazed to see how Daniel had changed in the two years since she had seen him. He was so grown-up in many ways, yet there was a boy's touch to some things. She told Dan a Mrs. Ward, an old friend from Mississippi, was coming over for tea and she would like Dan to stay and meet her. Dan thought the cakes would taste better with coffee and Aunt Ethel said she thought that could be arranged.

Mrs. Ward arrived at 4 P.M. and had her six-year-old daughter with her. Mrs. Ward explained she had accompanied her new husband who was trying to get an appointment with someone in the war department. She was busy discussing the local gossip with Ethel which left Dan and her child to fend for themselves. She said her name was Mary Jane Golden. When Mary Jane saw Dan had coffee, she asked if she could have some, only she wanted it loaded with cream and sugar. Dan had the cook fix her a cup of coffee and passed her the plate of cookies; she responded, "Thank you Mr. Wootton." Dan was startled since it was the first time anyone had addressed him as Mr. Wootton. He reflected this child looked upon him in his uniform as a grown-up. He asked about her name being Golden and she told him her father had died three years ago and her mother had recently married Mr. Ward. Mary Jane accepted Dan's expression of sympathy by saying she did not remember much about it except her father had been ill for a long time and he liked to have her brought to his bed. She remembered he liked to invent games for them to play. She said she thought things would be better now that Mr. Ward was her stepfather. Dan had her wrap three of the cookies in her handkerchief to take with her as they left.

Ethel Johns asked Dan how long he could stay and Dan replied his pass was good until noon tomorrow, Friday. He did not think they would be in Richmond much beyond that. There were rumors about where they were going but none of them said anything about staying in Richmond for very long. Ethel Johns told the cook to fix a good supper for them and to have the guest room turned down for him.

Dan thought, "I'll enjoy a real bed again; let's see when was I in a bed last?"

His great aunt, who he called aunt, led him into discussing his experiences in leaving home and in the training he had received. She hoped he could come back Sunday and go to church with her and Dan said he would be back or get word to her he could not. He mentioned the little girl who had startled him by calling him as "Mr. Wootton." Aunt Ethel said it may have been new to Dan but Dan had matured so much he should find it was common from now on; to a little girl of six, he would appear to be well into his twenties.

Dan slept as though he had been drugged. He woke well after daylight when he heard the cook stirring the fire. He stretched and rolled in the soft bed thinking his army bedroll had not been too bad until he spent the night in Ethel's good home. The old bedroll and a roommate nearby somehow did not seem as good as it once did. The cook had a pot of hot coffee and all the trimmings when he got out to the dining room.

She fed him and said, "Miss Johns won't be down for an hour or more so why don't you read the *Richmond Despatch* and I'll keep the coffee cup full."

When Aunt Ethel came down for breakfast, Dan took his leave with sincere thanks for altering his uniform and the great food and good night's sleep. He promised to return for Sunday services and dinner or get a note to her that he couldn't get leave.

Saturday, Dan sent his aunt a note saying again, thank you for a great time. I do not know where we are going but we have orders to move.

CHAPTER V

First Post

DEAR Grandpa Johns:

These have been busy days for us but they seemed to have slowed up some since we've settled in Norfolk. We were mustered in on May 18 and left Garysburg for Richmond on May 22 and received orders to move on the 25th. We loaded everything on the cars and waited for goodness knows what. We found out on our first move from Warrenton to Garysburg we should be prepared with food to take with us on the train but on the move from Richmond the ladies of the Richmond churches gave us a fine dinner. They came out in their buggies and were loaded with baskets of fried chicken and all kinds of good things. I don't know how they heard about us being stuck on the cars with only cold food but their efforts to provide us with something good to eat not only tasted good; it broke up a boring Sunday.

Sometime late Sunday night we got started and it was still quite dark when we landed here at Norfolk. I don't think that we'll be here at Ward's farm for very long because Captain Wade is scouting another location near Sewell's Point at what they call Camp Fisher. It's only seven miles from where we now are so it'll not be so much of a move.

You may remember I stayed with a young lawyer by the name

of Peter Spruill when I first went to Warrenton and he became the company sergeant. He is a real fellow and I'm disturbed at the treatment he has been given. He has been reduced in rank to a private and left here in the company. He's been sick quite often and has tried to get his job done when he did not feel like doing anything. The payoff was an accusation he was not strict enough with his men and his actions might damage the unit's effectiveness; hence, they decided he must be reduced in rank. There is nothing any of us can do but we feel an injustice has been done.

They tell us the Yankees are only twelve miles away at Fort Monroe and I'm sure we have nothing with us that can dislodge them and so far they haven't shown any interest in trying to run us out of here. You've read they tried to destroy everything here as they left but they did not really destroy the base. Some of our people think they can salvage the ship they tried to burn.

I don't think I ever gave you a rundown on our company as it got going. We started on April 18 with forty-seven men and gained thirty-eight more on April 29, picked up six more before we left for Garysburg, and twelve more before we left Garysburg for Richmond. That makes 103 for now. As you might guess we have more people who were farmers than anything else; we do have lawyers, dentists, cabinetmakers, a deputy sheriff, merchants, salesman, teachers and wainwrights. About what you would expect from the area where we lived. The farmers as a group seem to adapt most readily and seem to be the most resourceful when we have to make do with what we have.

My guess is we'll be in the area for some time and we could be in a lot worst shape. The climate is good and the seafood, as you know, is great. Say hello to everyone for me and I am sure you'll share this with Mom and Dad.

Love,
Dan

*

Dan and his friends made their camp into a comfortable place for their stay. They pulled guard duty every third day but their life was pleasant by most standards. They liked the chance to get acquainted with the people in town and the weather was pleasant with occasional showers that served to keep the day fresh and cool. The company was shocked on June 14 when Peter Spruill became very ill and he was transferred to the general hospital in Richmond. They learned he died on Tuesday, June 25.

Dan and the rest of the company felt they had suffered a loss of a kind friend who had many talents but admittedly was not made to be the world's best soldier. It would have been bad enough if he had died because of enemy action. His being sacked as their sergeant and then his death from camp fever made everyone think some how justice had gone astray. He became a victim of camp fever when they were at Garysburg and never really was back in full control since then. No one had expected he would die from camp fever, no matter how distressing and uncomfortable it made you feel. Their anger turned to Lieutenant Bennett who they blamed for his handling of the demotion. This anger carried onward to when the company elections were scheduled and they promptly turned down his re-election.

Captain Wade brought the company back to the normal state of morale by a series of training exercises and a marked change in their diet and in the camp's sanitation. The training exercises put their minds and energy to work on learning more sophisticated commands and maneuvers. The exercises took on the realistic fighting effort that had not been more than touched upon in their previous short training periods. It covered forced marches and great attention on how to take cover and still maintain contact and exercises that taught them how to survive on the water and the rations they could carry.

Captain Wade also made for a supply of fresh food and had an oven built. That gave the cooks a way of baking which coupled with the supply of seafood from the Chesapeake Bay made their meals seem like something that never existed in the army. The improvement in their diet and the training they received in sanitation cut the camp fever incidence and brought the company back to its normal exuberance. It also made the personnel feel they had the best company commander of anyone in the regiment.

The company was thrilled with the news of the battle of Manassas on Saturday and Sunday, July 20 and 21. The paper's report of the disastrous retreat of McDowell's troops back to Washington convinced many the war was about over. The governors of several states refused to accept any more volunteers for service since they clearly were not needed and there was no need to incur the expense of raising and equipping more troops.

There was generally pleasant news for the summer of 1861 except the loss of the fort at Cape Hatteras. Dan had a short leave to visit his Aunt Ethel in Richmond and learned from her that some shortages were being felt. His aunt complained that the price of good tea and coffee was getting to be ridiculous. The blockade was not effective but the price was being forced up by the speculators who were using the blockade as an excuse. The ladies of his aunt's circle were busy sewing and knitting for the troops. Dan could not understand why the ladies thought President Davis was a great man but thought Mrs. Davis was not a satisfactory first lady.

In October, came the first signal that maybe it wasn't going to be as short a war as they had thought. They moved into winter quarters at Camp Arrington on Sewell's Point. It was a good thing they got the move finished before the storm hit on November 2. Dan thought it was the worst storm he had ever seen and it blew for three days. The campground they had just left was not only flooded but was so badly washed they would surely have lost equipment if not men. A great fleet of Federal troops were at sea preparing for an invasion on the North Carolina coast when the storm struck. Ships and cargo were destroyed; in one location, 600 horses were washed ashore and an entire ship and crew were captured.

The weather in November was bad and was followed by even

worse weather in December and January. Again, a great Federal fleet on the way to attack Roanoke Island was damaged in the February storms but not enough to prevent Burnside from capturing Roanoke Island and throwing terror into the population along the North Carolina coast. Dan had observed the work going on at the naval base since shortly after his company had been shipped to Sewell's Point. They had been able to raise the ship, *Merrimac*, that the Federals thought they had destroyed as they withdrew. On March 8, the *Merrimac*, which had been renamed the *Virginia*, was ready to go, having been refitted as an ironclad and with an enormous cast-iron prow that extended four feet. Dan had watched the test runs and it looked like the deck was almost awash but the crew were happy with the results. They got steam up Saturday morning and went down the Elizabeth River about noon with troops lining the banks and cheering as she passed by.

The trip was supposed to be a test run and what a test run it turned out to be. The crew knew that she drew twenty-two feet and her engines were her weakness but she was as ready as she was going to be so off they took her into the channel. Her draft meant she had to stay in the Hampton Roads main channel and her speed and steering left ample room for improvement. She headed for Newport News where the *Congress* and the *Cumberland* were moored near the protection of that strong fortification. No one paid any attention to the *Virginia* until she got within three quarters of a mile. Both the *Congress* and the *Cumberland* tried to clear for action and get under way as did the rest of the Federal fleet moored near Fortress Monroe. The *Virginia* held her fire until she got into close range and took out a gun and its crew on the *Congress* with her first volley. She turned and headed for the *Cumberland* and rammed her amidships, backed away and turned to finish the *Congress*. The *Cumberland* suffered a hole in her hull big enough to drive a wagon through but she continued to fight as she sank. The *Virginia* at two hundred yards could make every shot count and the *Congress* could not damage her adversary. When she surrendered, a try was made to take off her wounded but the fire from shore made that impossible and she had to be fired. It was now near five o'clock and with the tide ebbing, the decision was made to return to Sewell's Point instead of destroying the *Minnesota* who had tried to get into the fray and had grounded herself on the way to Newport News. It seem safe to assume she could be finished off the next morning. For what was supposed to be a trial run, it had been a good day.

Dan and the rest of the troops could not see the action except the smoke from the fires but they could hear the cannonading and they learned about the great trial run when the *Virginia* docked and started to prepare for the next day's work. They were up early Sunday to cheer the *Virginia* on as she steamed out to take care of the *Minnesota* and the rest of the Federal fleet. They could hear the sound of gunfire for several hours but did not see the smoke from the expected fires. When the *Virginia* docked near evening, they learned about the battle with the Federal ironclad, the *Monitor*. It had been expected for sometime and arrived to protect the *Minnesota*. The *Monitor* had retired to shallow waters about two o'clock where the *Virginia* could not follow. The main damage to the *Virginia* was to the smoke stack which hampered her ability to make steam and they had not been able to see any damage to the *Monitor*. At one point in the battle, the captain could not understand why shots were not being fired and upon inquiry, the gunner reported he was running short on powder and shot and he had found he could cause as much damage to the *Monitor* as she came into range by snapping his fingers, so he had resorted to that mode of attack.

Dan, his friends and the whole South were thrilled to learn what Lieutenant John M. Brooke had been able to do with an old ship that had been abandoned and fired by the Federals because she was not worth taking with them as they left Newport.

Most of the other news was not good. Again, there was a fierce storm off the coast on May 3 and 4. Dan could hardly believe it but their orders came through to pack everything and be ready to move on Monday, May 6. They got their gear aboard early and waited, as they were finding to be the usual rule, for the engine and the crew to move them to Petersburg. The next day they heard the sad news the *Virginia* had been run aground and destroyed which left both the York and the James rivers open to the Federals.

Dear Grandpa:

I haven't had time to write to anyone since we left Newport and as usual I forgot you did not know I'm no longer in Newport. You cannot believe the things that have happened in the last two months. It took an amazing amount of effort to get here from Newport to where we are now at Malvern Hill. First, I thought we had seem some bad storms this last winter but nothing compared with the gully washer we had the first few days of May. We were delayed some by the storm but managed to get everything aboard the train and got into St. Petersburg on May 5.

Before we left Sewell's Point, we had to reorganize because we all enlisted for one year. The Conscription Act of April, 1862 required that we enlist for three years or the duration. This meant we should have elections as we did the year earlier. We re-elected Captain Wade and at almost the same time he was appointed to lieutenant colonel and attached to the field staff of the regiment. It was bittersweet for us as we wanted to see our Captain Wade get the recognition we thought he deserved but we hated to lose our friend and captain. We had elected Nat Harmon as our first lieutenant and he moved to captain as Ben Wade moved on. As I told you in an earlier letter, most of us felt Isham Bennett was in some measure responsible for Peter Spruill's problems that led to his death. He had been elected as our second lieutenant in April, 1861 and he was resoundingly defeated for re-election. We replaced him with John Turnbull who is a good man who joined when I did on April 18, 1861. He was a merchant before he entered the service with us.

We don't know why we were so rapidly yanked out of Newport but maybe you have more information on that than we do. It really was dream duty at Sewell's Point and from what we have been learning lately, it could not have lasted. We hear the *Virginia* was run aground and destroyed which must leave the Federals in complete control of the York and the James rivers. A court of inquiry is to be convened. It'll not bring back all the hard work and skill that Lt. Brooke and his men spent in getting an old wreck in condition to scare the daylights out of the Federals. We seem to have many talented men but the general results do not seem to match our expectations.

Anyhow, the train got us to St. Petersburg where we were detached from Mahone's brigade and assigned to General Branch's brigade at Gordonsville and shortly after we arrived there, the whole brigade was transferred to Ashland. We stood picket duty watching the Federals at Fredericksburg and in front of Richmond. Some of our regiment had a skirmish near Hanover Courthouse and then the whole brigade was pulled back to Ashland. We were transferred back to Mahone's brigade and then shortly after setting up in front of Richmond, we were transferred to General Samuel Garland's brigade. General Garland's command was and is a part of General D. H. Hill's Division. We think that Generals Garland and Hill are top-grade military men but boy have they taught us what shank's mare means. I was five foot ten inches and weighed 150 pounds when I entered service and may have lost some of that by now. Those boots you sent me are worth their weight in gold. Thank Sam for a job well done.

We moved out and were on the road at 2 A.M. on June 26, that is a Thursday, I think. About 4 P.M. a part of General Hill's Division was in action supporting the troops concentrating under General R.E. Lee but we did not get into any part of the day's action; marching but no firing. Before daylight on Friday we were on our way again, this time to join General Jackson's troops on the left of our lines; we had been brought up on the right by Thursday's march. After a little more than an hour's march, there was enough light for General Hill to see our way was blocked by Federal troops. General Hill sent our brigade and one other to the left to take them by flank and rear attack. The Federals really took off when they saw what we had in store for them and we went on to Cold Harbor. After General Jackson's troops came up, we had a sharp fight with Federals but we forced them from the woods.

During the night, the Federals withdrew and we moved across the Chickahominy River where we found the Federals had destroyed the bridges. It took us two days to rebuild the bridges. I learned a lot about bridge building in these two days and believe me, it's hard work. The general had ordered his staff to prepare the plans for the bridge but the old man in our outfit got us started because he had been a carpenter. When we finished, he went to the General and said, "General, I'm still waiting for the plans but your bridge is finished."

On June 30, we crossed the Chickahominy and found the White Oak Bridge had been destroyed and the Federals were contesting our rebuilding efforts. We were held at that point until they were threatened by a force after the battle of Frayser's Farm. We quickly rebuilt the bridge and advanced to meet the enemy here at Malvern Hill. On the afternoon of July 1, we were in the center of the attack on the Federal position which meant we had to advance across open fields with the Federal artillery about 700 yards in front of our take-off point. We were forced to halt and take cover and our support did not come up, so we had to retire at dusk. The next morning we found the enemy had retired to Harrison's Landing on the James River where he had the protection of his gun boats.

This has been much hard work and sometimes it seemed the demands were more than we could cope with but we have also had some thrilling times when we could prevail against the enemy. In the last few days, we have lost some good men. It's the hardest thing we have to carry. We have lost eight good men in the two fights and have ten wounded. Some wounded may be lost to us. Richard Davis, for one, is a good friend and has been with us from the first day at Warrenton. He taught me about bridge building just a few days ago on the Chickahominy and he may live but I doubt he will be able to return to the service. I'm sure we would have had more casualties but for the time we had at Newport where Captain Wade put us through the training program for what we now are doing.

This has been a long letter but there has been many things happening and I've tried to fill you in on what we are doing. You and Dad will have more insight into what's going on and how what I see fits into the moves both sides are making. Hope we have a chance to talk about it some day soon but I don't have any idea when I can get leave. At the moment, they're not giving out any leaves and I am sure we will be moving on from here.

Love, Dan.

CHAPTER VI

Maryland

DAN'S brigade stayed at Malvern Hill for eight days which they spent in getting the troops back in shape and in refitting the companies. On July 10, they were marched back to their Richmond base. In mid-August, they were moved to Hanover Junction and on August 26 they were marched to Orange Court House. They left there on August 28 and arrived in Chantilly, Virginia (near the southeast corner of the present day Dulles airport) after the second battle of Manassas. They crossed into Maryland on September 4.

The company had to learn some new tricks. This fellow Lee was now the General in command of the Army of Northern Virginia and he had some different ideas about what an army should do. First, he thought they should attack at every opportunity instead of holding on and trying to defend a fixed position. He had definite ideas they should learn how to move without much excess baggage. They struck their tents and left them at the camp at Orange Court House plus many other housekeeping paraphernalia they had accumulated. And did he teach them to march. They thought they were in good shape but they soon found this fellow gave them sore muscles they did not know they had. They learned they could cover more miles than they would have thought possible and to survive on the food they could carry in their knapsack.

While Dan and his fellow infantry men thought they were walking their legs off, the artillery men rode on their caissons. There was much comment about this between the troops. The artillery men called the infantry "crunchers" and Dan's group said at least they did not have to look at the wrong end of a horse all day. Lee, one day, observed the artillery men riding and promptly brought a halt to their riding. The artillery men made more noise about having to walk than they did about leaving their tents at Orange Court House.

They marched to Frederick and camped about two miles out of town on the Hagerstown Road. They had a few days to recover from their ten days of stressful marching and then after five days of hot food, they were on the march, again, to Boonsboro on Wednesday, September 10. They were detailed to guard the passes, so Jackson could complete the task of taking Harpers Ferry without danger of Federal attack to his rear.

Dan and his buddies were amused at one of the reasons for their thrust into Maryland. He discovered years later the camp gossip was true. Apparently, as the gossip reported, Jefferson Davis and others had thought the state of Maryland really wanted to be a part of the Confederacy and had been prevented from expressing their will by the iron fist the Federals used. They assumed if the Confederate army appeared, there would be a grand rush to enlist and maybe cause the Federal capitol to be moved. When the army camped at Frederick, there were printed proclamations distributed to the townspeople suggesting this "friendly" army was there to help the citizens of Maryland. Lee had issued specific instructions they were to pay for anything they took; pay being in Confederate paper money or with certificates of indebtedness. Both Lee and Davis' headquarters group were amazed they got a cold reaction to the proclamation and an even chillier belief they were being compensated for the "purchases" of supplies, horses and food.

Dan and his company were not concerned with how the people were paid for the food and clothes but they sure liked hot food and especially the eggs they were enjoying. A chance to get a bath and to get some clean clothes made the troops feel like they were ready for the next adventure and as they left Frederick, people were happy to see them go and had to admit they looked better as they left than they did when they came into town and for certain, they smelled a lot better.

There were three passes to be guarded near Boonsboro and General D.H. Hill put his troops into the two principal passes and the third was blocked by a small detachment of cavalry. For some reason, the regimental officers were not present when Dan's brigade was sent to support the Fifth Regiment and some troops broke and ran when they received heavy fire. Dan's company joined the Fifth and fought with them for the rest of the day. Their own regimental commander, General Garland, was killed at some point in the battle on September 14 and was replaced by Colonel McRae from the Fifth South Carolina who led the regiment as it was withdrawn to Sharpsburg along the Antietam Creek.

The bloodiest battle in history happened here on the 17th, 26,000 killed. The regiment still under the command of Colonel McRae was held in reserve until about ten o'clock when they were ordered to support the left which was being pressed by McClellan's troops. They advanced to the woods and then formed a battle line. They received a series of conflicting orders followed by an order to cease fire because they were thought to be firing into their own troops. About this time the enemy appeared on their right flank and the troops fled. Later most of the brigade was rallied by Colonel Iverson and others and returned to the support of the center, giving useful service. Although there was savage fighting here and at the passes near Boonsburo, Dan and his company did not suffer a wound or anyone killed. The brigade was not as fortunate, they had 40 killed, 210 wounded, and 187 missing. The two armies rested where they were on Thursday, September 18. At night, General Lee withdrew the army across the Potomac.

Dan's company again had a chance to rest and recoup and to get some hot food. Coffee was getting hard to find and the value of the Confederate money had started to deteriorate. Dan was more fortunate than most of the others because he had a good pair of boots going into these marches. Some people in his company had to manage with shabby footwear; a fact General Lee had noticed before they started the campaign and throughout the rest of the war was to beg President Davis to do something to supply the footwear the troops needed.

As they rested in the Shenandoah Valley at various locations, Dan's company was camped where the two forks of the Shenandoah River came together; from that point, they could guard the passes into the valley. The Army of Northern Virginia recovered 20,000 people that had not been able to sustain the demanding pace set by Lee. These were people that could not keep pace because they did not have shoes or adequate shoes, who found a warm bed and decided life was better there for a few days, people that really were too old for the type of campaign Lee was demanding, and people who thought that they would live longer or better if they dodged their duty. There were some who deserted and could not be persuaded to return to service; there were many tries made to find them and bring them to justice as Lee termed it. There was more than a little conviction this was turning into a rich man's war and a poor man's fight. Lee and the rest of the officer corps took a hard line stand on anyone who straggled as they termed it. They did not think there was any valid reason for someone to drop out of the line of march. Lee appealed to Davis to secure passage of a law that would permit a court to follow the army, conduct trials on location and make for summary execution of the sentences. The fact the officer corps rode horseback or in an ambulance and had servants to establish camp for them did not make the troops think their officers really understood the problem. The fact that 20,000 troops would take the trouble to find their old units and return to service on their own did not impress the officer corps; the one bad apple was more visible than the ten that returned.

On November 6, the regiment got their new General. He was General Alferd Iverson who had been promoted to a brigadier general and assigned to their brigade, the Twelfth. This was the same man who as a colonel had rallied them at Sharpsburg after the struggle they had with confusing and contradictory orders from McRae. They were moved to Culpeper Courthouse, then pulled back to Strasburg, moved to Gordonsville on November 21, to Fredericksburg and then on December 3 they were marched to Port Royal to prevent a crossing of the Rappahannock River. As the battle developed at Fredericksburg, they were ordered back there on December 12; and on December 13, took their position in the third defensive line. During the battle Saturday, they were subjected to heavy artillery fire but otherwise, saw little action. They were advanced to the second line the next day and to the first line where they stayed Monday and Tuesday. While on this assignment, they were not engaged but had five men wounded by artillery fire. After the battle, they went into winter quarters near Fredericksburg and did picket duty along the Rappahannock River.

CHAPTER VII

Pennsylvania

*D*EAR Grandpa:

You know where I've been and what I've been doing I'm sure but as I look back on the last seven months, I can hardly believe we did cover the ground and do all those things. This is getting to be a bad war. Some boys we captured at Sharpsburg had been on a farm less than a month before they were in a tough fight. For the training and the type of officers they had, they did better than could have been expected. There was an amazing number who died at Sharpsburg before they could learn how to be a soldier. The one thing where they had us at a disadvantage was in artillery. They're beginning to out-gun us in this area and it may get to be serious.

Before I forget, let me thank you, again, for having Sam make those boots for me. They were real lifesavers on this run we made into Maryland. You should see what pitiful quantity and quality of shoes that we get. Something's wrong because this man's army isn't getting the supplies and the material we must have if we are to win. There are times we would be in real trouble for food except for the generosity of the ladies in the area. We think well of Generals Lee and Jackson and Hill but they cannot seem to get the supplies and equipment we need. We think our generals stand a lot taller than

McClellan, Burnside, Pope and their peers. This fellow Jackson and our own Hill think we can move like no army ever has. I would not know if it's true but we have marched more miles in fewer days than I would have ever thought possible. I thought you and I used to do a good walking job when we were out hunting but we did not come close to what this fellow has put us through.

We are in winter quarters here at Fredericksburg and have to stand picket duty on the river. From the looks of things, I don't think the Federals will try anything in this cold weather and I don't think Lee can get enough supplies together to make a march.

If you can, have Sam make me another pair of boots. I'm all right at the moment but I expect we will be back marching when the weather breaks. We have a shoemaker from Warrenton who volunteered shortly after I did and he helps keep our shoes and boots repaired but he is limited in what he can find and in the tools he has. I think he'll be discharged soon; he is just too old to maintain the pace we have to meet. I think he's in his forties. The way this fellow Stonewall Jackson moves us around, John Harris (our shoemaker) will never make it and it will be better to have him making shoes and boots instead of being killed or captured because he cannot march.

General D. H. Hill is being transferred to a larger job in Richmond and we hate to see him leave. His successor is General Edward Johnson who is absent wounded now and we will have General Robert E. Rodes, the Brig-gen of the First Brigade, taking his place until General Johnson can return to service.

Our General Garland was killed near Boonsboro, as I'm sure you have read in the papers. We had some rough times when a Colonel tried to take over and run the brigade. He couldn't seem to get clear orders to the field commanders. We didn't do as good a job as some other units. Had it not been for efforts of our current General Iverson, then a colonel, on the last day at Sharpsburg, we might have been killed or captured. We think that he's a knowledgeable and a courageous officer.

The report we get is that General Burnside is to be removed from command because of his errors at Fredericksburg and a General Joe Hooker'll be his replacement. We guess it'll be some time before Hooker'll want to move because they lost too much with Burnside and it's very cold here. I assume it's at home, too. You can peel the skin from your hands in a hurry in this weather.

Love to all. Tell them to write whenever they can.

Dan

Dan's company stayed in winter quarters at Fredericksburg until the last part of April. It was a bitterly cold winter with more snow than the old timers in the area could remember seeing before. On April 29, the brigade was ordered to march to Hamilton's Crossing below Fredericksburg. This extended the right side of the Confederate line to Massaponax Creek. The troops while there on April 29 and 30 were subjected to occasional shelling but no general action followed. General Lee ordered the division back to Hamilton's Crossing during the evening of the 30th because he thought the activity at Massaponax was a feint. On May 1, General Jackson moved his troops to meet an attack by General Hooker from the direction of Chancellorsville. Dan's brigade was in the lead as they swung out on the march, the same as they had been last September. They found the enemy had been engaged about three miles from Chancellorsville and they were placed in position on the right. When the enemy retired, Dan's brigade was ordered to hold their position and at nightfall were withdrawn from the line. They marched to within a mile of Chancellorsville and camped for the night. At daylight, they were ordered to relieve a brigade on the line and then at 10 A.M., they joined with another division to flank the Federal position. With hard marching, they did reach a point about four miles west of Chancellorsville where they were on the exposed right flank of Hooker's army. The Federals seemed totally surprised and broke and ran. The hungry Confederates grabbed food and ammunition as they passed through the enemy camp and took after the fleeing troops of Hooker. The Federal Calvary tried to halt their advance but were driven off. That night the brigades were reformed and Dan's took the third line for the next day's battle.

There was sharp fighting the next day, May 3 and Dan's brigade had to help a brigade on their right that was nearly flanked but generally the Federals continued to retreat and after they had recrossed the Rappahannock, Dan's brigade was returned to their old camp at Fredericksburg. Dan's regiment lost twelve killed, ninety-six wounded and eleven missing or captured. Dan's company had seven wounded. The real loss for Dan and the whole Army was the wounding and later death of Stonewall Jackson. The regiment also lost their acting commander, Major David Pinkney Rowe.

Following the Chancellorsville battles, Lee regrouped his forces into three corps and Dan's unit (Iverson's brigade) became a part of Major General Rode's division which was a part of Lieutenant General Ewell's Second Corp. They spent nearly a month getting their equipment back in order and the soreness out of their muscles when they began to hear rumors something big was being planned. Dan was sure that it meant more marching for long hours on dusty roads and he was glad that he had received his new boots and had a chance to break them in.

Sure enough, on June 3 they broke camp and set off with Dan's brigade leading the way. They marched to Culpeper Court House and a little beyond by June 7. So far, the pace of their march had not been as bad as it had been the last time when they had turned west and north. The rumor this time was they were on their way to Pennsylvania to see if they could not find better forage and supplies for their needs and to take the pressure off the Richmond line. First, they had to back track ten miles at forced march when the Federal cavalry made a determined attack on Stuart's cavalry at Brandy Station. The Federals had left when the brigade got there and they retraced their steps.

They resumed their march to the Shenandoah Valley and on Friday, June 12 they were ordered to go to Cedarville through Chester Gap. They received orders to go to Berrysville and Martinsburg; the rest of the army moved against the enemy at Winchester. They reached Berrysville on June 13 but the Federal force there left ahead of their arrival. On Sunday, June 14 they charged the troops at Martinsburg. They drove the enemy through the town and for two miles beyond town at forced march pace. The infantry made good their escape because Rodes was concentrating on the enemy's artillery and cavalry. On Monday, they heard about the victory at Winchester and they moved to Williamsport to wait for the rest of the force to catch up with them. They had time to rest until Friday when they marched out in front on the road to Hagerstown. They had been nearby the previous September and stayed here for two days this time. On Monday, June 22 they marched out to Greencastle, Pennsylvania and Dan observed their food got better the further north they marched.

They moved to Chambersburg and passed through town on June 24 and were joined by the force under General Johnson. Together, they went to Carlisle where they arrived on Saturday night. From there, Rode's division moved on down the valley to Heidlersburg. Dan thought the farmland was beautiful and the food seemed to be plentiful and good. After they had made camp, Dan walked to a nearby farm to look at the fields and the barns. The farmer came out to see what he wanted and Dan told him what a good farm he had. He said it reminded him of his Grandfather Johns farms in Virginia. The old Dutchman was surprised a soldier just wanted to look instead of steal something and was amazed at Dan's youth and the distance he had traveled. He could see this boy would like a good hot meal and it was probable he could stand a good bath. He asked Dan if he would like a hot meal of scrambled eggs, sausage, potatoes, and hot biscuits. He did not have to repeat the offer.

The old Dutchman yelled for his hired girl, Hilda, to tell Mama they would have a visitor for supper and to bring some clothes Max had left when he went into service.

"Max," he said, "was my hired hand and he was about your size and I think you could do with a warm bath and a change of clothes. Hilda will fix a tub in the barn and you can get a good soaking before Hilda finishes the milking and Mama gets supper ready."

Hilda set the wash tub on boards and brought the clothes, the soap, towel, and hot water. Dan closed the barn door and slipped out of the worn dirty jeans he had marched in for days. He could not remember how long that it had been since he had a warm bath. He scrubbed with the good old home-made soap he remembered from his own home. Before he got out to dry, he slumped down to enjoy the warm soapy water and the next thing he knew he heard the barn door opening. Hilda entered saying he must have fallen asleep. Dan was so warm and relaxed that he thought he could have slipped off for a few minutes.

Hilda said, "Let me wash your back the way I used to wash Max's."

Dan asked, "What happened to Max?

Hilda said, "He got himself killed less than a month after he went into service. That is why we have his clothes here; he never wrote or came back for them and he had no family. Now step out on this board and let me dry you off with this towel."

As Hilda rubbed Dan's muscular body with the towel, he began to get a sensation he had never felt before. It was as warm and pleasing as it was strange and new. Hilda nearly finished drying when she noticed the excitement she had created. She dropped the towel and her drawers and pulled Dan down on top of her in the hay. It was over almost immediately after it started and now Dan knew what the fellows had been talking about ever since he entered the service. It was pleasant but not the everything his buddies had told him it was. As Hilda cleaned herself and then Dan, the urge returned and this time Dan helped push Hilda into the hay. It lasted a little longer and finished with a demanding surge.

Hilda said they should get to the house for supper and to let her go first with the milk and she would tell them he had been asleep and would be right up. Hilda said she and Max used to have much fun. Why didn't Dan stay and work on the farm?

Dan said it really didn't matter now what he might like to do because he was in the army and had to complete the work as he was ordered. Even if he tried to leave, the forces from both armies would be on the lookout for him and each one would as soon shoot him as look at him. Even General Lee has tried to get permission to shoot the people who fell out because they cannot maintain the pace Lee has demanded from us.

Dan would long remember the pleasant two hours on the farm near Heidlersburg; the good farm food, the well-tended fields and the only good coffee he had in over a year. This made him wonder if what he had been doing for two years was really worth the strain and the pain that had been needed. "Anyway it had been a good way to end the month of June and I wonder what tomorrow, Wednesday, July 1, 1863 will have in store for us. Should I go back to the farm if we'll be here for a few days?"

Dan did not have to answer the question because when he got to his company camp he found everyone was putting the gear and provisions in order for a forced march the next morning. It seemed a detachment of Confederate troops had started to Gettysburg where they had heard they would find a warehouse full of shoes. They found a Federal force and General Hill had ordered General Ewell to move to either Cashtown or Gettysburg as the need might arise. They were on their way early and had not been on the road two hours when a courier arrived and directed they go to Gettysburg to support Hill. When they arrived they found Hill's men were already engaged and they moved into position on Hill's left. General Early's division arrived shortly after Ewell's and with Hill's force they drove the Federals through the town of Gettysburg.

There was sharp fighting all afternoon as the Federals were not ready to run. The loss on both sides was heavy and Dan's troop blocked the retreat of several companies of Federals trying to escape along the railroad tracks. The Federals retreated to defensive positions south of town where Dan's unit tried to dislodge them from the top of Culp's Hill. There was natural cover for the Federals' protection which made progress up the hill nearly impossible and as dusk came on Dan's unit regrouped near the base of Culp's Hill. They were out of ammunition and had to resort to checking bodies on the field for their supply. Dan hoped they would get some food and water and they must have their supply wagons bring up more ammunition.

They got water and ammunition during the night and had to make do with the food they carried with them. They had been able to hear the Federals all during the night as they were moving rocks into place to strengthen their positions. Dan and his buddies thought it was tough enough trying to go up that hill yesterday; it would be a disaster to try it now. Nonetheless, before daylight they were ordered to prepare for the assault up the hill. It was real slaughter for an Alabama and a South Carolina brigade and Dan's brigade was ordered to retreat. They did get a hot meal as they returned to camp on July 2.

Among the other tragedies they heard about, was the story of young Culp who had enlisted in the Confederate service when the war broke out. He had served all during the war with no wounds. He was thrilled to see his grandfather's farm but the next day, a Yankee bullet killed him instantly. For some reason this loss of a young life cast a somber cloud over everyone, although there were hundreds of others that were equally tragic. What a foolish waste in trying to storm up Culp's Hill against a well-prepared position. Dan could not believe it when they were told they would attack again, on Friday, July 3.

This time their plan of attack was better. It opened with an intense cannon fire from the Confederate batteries and after two hours of this attack, Dan's units started to move out. They took advantage of the rocks and trees that gave some protection for their advance, while the cannoning continued. They got to positions to storm the line when the cannons stopped and word was passed to attach bayonets and watch for the signal to charge. They charged across the remaining distance and met a blast of firepower from both rifles and cannon. They almost carried the day when they had to retreat and seek cover. As Dan was trying to make the cover of a large boulder, he felt a sharp blow to the calf of his right leg and he rolled on over the boulder as he passed out from the pain.

Dan did not know how long he had been out when he came to but it was evening and strangely quiet. He took stock of his situation. His leg did not seem to hurt too much but it was completely numb. He could not get his muscles to move it. He could hear other people groaning and some in the distance crying but could not identify any other sounds. He was close enough to the Federal lines he should have heard their conversations, unless they too had withdrawn. He looked around for his rifle and guessed it was on the other side of the boulder because he could not find it on this side. He used his knife to raise his cap over the boulder and when it did not draw fire he pulled himself around the boulder with his elbows. As far as he could tell, there was nothing around but the usual litter of a battle field including himself. There was a broken gun carriage near by and he decided he should try to get under it to protect from the cavalry as they rode across the area.

He took a long drink from his canteen and nearly drained it but there was no need to worry because the details would soon be out to gather the wounded and to bury the dead. He used his elbows to slide his body the few feet to the broken gun carriage. His wounded leg felt like it weighed a ton. He looked to see if it had caught on something but it was just the dead weight dragging its length on the ground. The gun carriage had one wheel damaged. The hub and the axle on one side were nearly on the ground. Dan pulled himself to a sitting position with the spokes of the one good wheel; he wanted to see the lights of the search parties and call to them. There were Yankee bodies all around the gun carriage and he assumed the Confederate artillery must have scored a direct hit on the unit. There were several Confederate bodies near the path he had traversed but no one nearby showed any signs of life, either Confederate or Yankee. He could not see any signs of the Federal lines and he could not make out any camp fires for the Confederate lines. Maybe both sides had pulled back to stronger defensive positions as they had done last year at Sharpsburg. What really bothered was the sounds of the wounded now were getting louder. Some were crying, some were the most horrible groans Dan had heard and some were begging for water. As the night drew on, Dan looked first where he thought his own lines were and could not find any sign of search parties and then he scanned the other direction but could not see any light moving showing that search parties were on the field.

He slept fitfully during the night; he would wake and look to what he thought was the direction of both lines but could not see anything moving. He became wide awake with daylight and found nothing that he could see or hear except the cries of the wounded. He found he would stare for what seemed like hours and then awake with a start not knowing he had been asleep. He thought there must be some reason they are waiting until nightfall to get their search parties out. He felt he could stay awake when the sun went down because he had napped during the day. He must have dropped off to sleep and awoke with a start as a sharp clap of thunder rolled across the hill. There was thunder and lightning as a prelude to the heaviest rain Dan had ever seen. He thought the rains on the coast in early 1862 were as bad as they could get. It rained and continued raining until Dan thought it would never stop. He wondered if it was catching any of the wounded in low spots for they would drown with this rain. He did not have anything he could use to catch water but he could twist around and get water as it cascaded off the gun carriage.

The rain broke about daylight and Dan pulled himself up as high as he could get to see if any of his field parties were moving onto the battle field. He could not see any movement and shortly he heard the familiar drum beat as the last of Lee's army left the area on Sunday, July 5. Dan could not believe they would just march off and leave him. He slid back down the wheel and lay in the mud listening to the sound of his friends going home and not even coming out to tend to the wounded or bury the dead. Lee must have been sorely tried to adopt this tactic and must believe the safety of the remaining troops demanded this cruel and unusual act. Dan felt he had been abandoned by the world and if he survived it would at best be in a Federal prison. At that, he was in a better situation than most of the wounded left on the field. While all needed attention, Dan's wound had disabled him but did not seen to be as life-threatening as a chest wound would have been. The feeling was returning to his leg plus the pain but he could not use or control it.

He got his knife from the scabbard that was built into his boot and slit his pants to get a look at what had happened to him. The leg was a horrible thing to look at but it seemed to be a major bruise instead of a penetration wound. He surmised a minie ball had caught him about four inches below the knee and probably had broken or cracked his shin bone. As best he could tell, there was no misalignment of the bone; it seemed reasonable to assume he had a bad bone and muscle bruise and in due time he would be back on his feet, albeit in a Federal prison. He looked to the Federal lines and did not see any movement from that direction. My God, he thought; everyone has just walked off as though there was nothing left to do here.

Dan watched at periodic intervals and no one came onto the field. They had more rain as if the Gods were trying to wash them away and forget there were people here who needed help and the dead needed the respect of burial. Dan thought at least we buried young Culp here on his family's farm. I hope they will be able to find his grave after this rain. The cries of the wounded were faint and it seemed like some of them were stilled for good.

Dan could not believe it when no one came to the battle field on Monday. When day arrived on Tuesday, he decided if he was going to survive it would be because he did something about it instead of wait for the Federals who may have gone off trying to find out what Lee was doing. By now, he was getting hungry and he was going to need water as well. His leg was painful but bearable. He was worried about the loss of ability to move or control his right leg but maybe it would return. Anyway there was nothing he could do about it at the moment. The first thing he needed was food and water. If there was any he could get, it had to be on the dead bodies nearby. As much as he hated to do it, he would have to search the dead for food and water by pulling himself with his elbows. The first body he came to was an officer that still had his saber. Dan broke the hilt from the blade and using the blade on one side and the scabbard on the other, made a splint for his leg. The belt and strap made the binding for the splints. If his leg was broken, he should see it did not move at the break. The support of this unusual splint did not seem to ease his pain but it gave him confidence he could move around without doing more damage to himself. The officer's canteen was cut from his belt and Dan was pleased to hear the sound of liquid sloshing in it. He open the canteen and spit the liquid out in disgust. It was brandy and he started to discard the canteen when he thought, "Maybe it would help my wound if I poured some of this on it." It burned but seemed to help cleanse the wound. He went to two more bodies before he found a canteen with water and some hardtack.

Dan had never thought hardtack was very good but this time he thought it was a very good meal. Guess it makes a difference in how food tastes depending on just how hungry you really are. Tuesday became quite warm by afternoon and the wounded still living cried more and more for water. The stench from decaying bodies began to permeate the air.

Dan thought, "It is a good thing I ate this morning because I could not stomach food with that smell around. It is too late to try to crawl out of here tonight but by tomorrow I must try to get out of here and see if I can find help for myself and the rest of these poor devils." Dan crawled back to his gun carriage and spent a restless night with the wounded cries going on all night.

Wednesday dawned bright and clear and either the night's coolness or the slight breeze had decreased the horrible stench. Dan braced himself against the wheel and took a long drink from the canteen. If he was going to crawl off the hill, he would not be able to carry the canteen with him. If he had to have water before he found help, he would have to search bodies or just do without. He verified that the knife was in his boot scabbard because he was sure to need it in his crawl. Before he started, he pulled himself up using the wheel spokes to get a line of direction and to see if he could spot landmarks that might help steer him back to the little town of Gettysburg they had fought through nearly a week before. He wondered what had happened to the poor devils who had been living there when this major battle had developed around them. Maybe someone had returned if they had left or they might have hid in the cellars as the shooting sprayed through the town. Dan could not remember seeing much destruction as he came through town but then he was not really looking at the scenery as he went through. As he got his one good leg under him, he could turn and look down the hill to the town. He tried to see what the best line would be for him and what landmark he might find to guide him because it was not going to be a straight line with the rugged terrain he would have to travel. His heart came up into his throat as he saw there was smoke coming from one of the houses. There was someone in the town. He watched and watched as his spirits rose that at least there was someone else in the world. He started to slide back down and begin his crawl when he saw several people come out of the house and look like they were coming up the hill. He could not help crying out, though he knew they could not hear him.

CHAPTER VIII

Homefront, 1862

EARLY in 1862, the papers carried the news of President Tyler's death. Daniel had known the old boy and always thought highly of his abilities. No one had expected him to be president when he was picked to run as Harrison's vice-president and some people in the Whig party were in for a cruel shock when they found out their new president was a Jeffersonian Democrat. Their attempts to railroad their plans around him proved to be very disappointing. He had been elected to the Confederate Congress but his death on January 18 came before the Congress met.

The papers carried the accounts of the loss of the forts on the Ohio River and Davis had removed both Generals Floyd and Pillow from their command and had ordered a board of inquiry to examine their conduct at Forts Henry and Donelson. Tom thought this was a way of stalling until the public forgot about their mismanagement of their forces. In Tom's view, they should have been shot but Daniel pointed out the reason for the stall and hopeful short memories was the political realities of Floyd and Pillow. Both Davis and Lincoln have more political generals than they need; they hope they can find some who will fight or that the enemy will take care of the ones that will not. Here Davis has two on his hands that either will not or do not know how to fight and he has to walk carefully because he does not have a big enough political stick to do what he would like to do.

They were very heartened by the news of the conversion of the *Merrimac* into the *Virginia* and the success in Hampton Roads. Latter they received young Dan's letter that detailed how he and his companions had cheered as the *Virginia* went on a "trial run." Tom and Daniel hoped Davis would see that the South followed up on this development.

In May, Daniel got a copy of the Confederate constitution that he had been told was patterned after the Federal one. One glance at the documents told him it started from a much different premise. Instead of starting with "We, the people—" this started with "We, the deputies of sovereign and independent states——" Daniel and Tom mused it is no wonder that Davis has a problem trying to be president and commander-in-chief when each of the states believes they have a right to do as they see fit instead of what may be stemming from a central government.

Also, in May, the Richmond paper had published in 1861 that what we needed was a dictator (and indicated Davis was the man for the office) now published an editorial complaining Jefferson Davis treats all men, as though they were idiotic insects. They had to laugh at the intellectual reversal and believed it was real and not just a means of trying to sell papers.

They devoured the news of McClellan's promotion and the resultant campaign he directed against Richmond. They did not know that young Dan was involved in the action until they got his letter after the battle at Malvern Hill. They were thrilled he had been in the battles and had learned how to survive. They were distressed that the *Virginia* had been abandoned. It seemed they could get an appreciable advantage almost in hand and then were not able or not willing to follow up. Maybe, this was because they did not do adequate planning or did not believe they should press their advantages. They were not seizing their advantages; it may have stemmed from the "all we want is to be left alone" or from the concept we have to protect Richmond above all else.

Daniel and Tom were more than a little concerned with the news Lee was taking the army into Maryland. The idea that the state of Maryland would throw off the Federal yoke if Lee's army appeared and offered them a chance, seemed too ludicrous to be seriously considered by either Lee or Davis. And Maryland surely was not the place to go to replenish supplies. The Richmond papers gave glowing accounts of the great victory at Sharpsburg which Tom said should be discounted because Lee was retreating across the Potomac. In a few days, they read in the Federal papers about a great Federal victory at Antietam. Daniel and Tom decided there had been a large battle called Sharpsburg by the South and Antietam by the Federals and beyond that, they should wait to see just what had happened.

It took the better part of a week to began to get an accurate picture of what had happened with the Maryland invasion. The invitation for Maryland to discard the Federals was issued by Lee when he occupied Frederick. The fact that it was not worth the effort to have the proclamation printed must have caused someone to wonder how they ever came up with that idea. But, Daniel said no; it only means they will say "it wasn't my idea."

The loss by both sides turned out to be enormous. The South could not afford the losses and at best it was a tragedy for both the North and the South. This was brought home when Tom learned from his daughter-in-law that Major Tom Wootton Jr. had been killed. He had been promoted to a Major's rank about the time they moved out on the Maryland campaign. They later learned he was one of the 36,000 casualties that happened in the few days action.

By winter, they heard young Dan had survived the campaign but had begun to wonder about the progress of the war. Tom was afraid Stuart's raid into Pennsylvania which netted 1,000 needed horses would lead to the idea that an excursion there would be planned for the next summer. Surely, supplies of all kinds were beginning to be hard to come by and at a dear price when they could be found. The active cotton trade with the North did not make sense but it was a way for the North to get cotton and for the South to get medical supplies and other things that were not available by any other means. That the trade also dropped gold into the pockets of various generals and people who had friends in high places was overlooked, unless it became a public scandal.

Martha arranged that they should celebrate Christmas at the Wootton household and then bring in the new year at the Johns' home. All the slaves were brought to the house to receive an extra allotment of food and a supply of molasses and to salute the occasion with the traditional eggnog cup. The family felt these occasions made for the best of traditional Virginia life and they fervently hoped this would continue.

Daniel did not want to think aloud on this issue but he thought, it has already changed and it looks like we are in for more. The year, 1863, probably was to be the turning point of the war.

On January 3, they read about a great victory General Bragg had secured in Tennessee at Murfreesboro. Tom said he did not believe the report, though Bragg had some capable generals reporting to him. The source of the story seemed to be Bragg himself which made Tom even more skeptical the report could be read as anything more than that a major battle had happened. We should wait to see what the actual results were although they all hoped that the reports could be true.

On January 6, the papers carried the story Bragg was retreating. Tom thought this made for good news and sad news. The sad part was their cause had again showed they could get the major part of an operation done in a great fashion and fail the completion. The good news part of the story was Tom was right in his appraisal of Bragg's ability. The sad part was no matter how true Tom and his fellow officers were in their evaluation, the one that counted was made by Jeff Davis and he could not believe his friend was anything but a genius. Even after several of Bragg's generals refused to serve under him again, Davis was sure they were mistaken. About the same time they heard Lincoln had issued his Emancipation Proclamation, although it was not printed in any of their papers. In the same week, they heard the *Monitor* had sunk as it was being towed away from Hampton Roads. The new and astounding item was the Federal Congress approval of the use of Negro troops. They just could not believe anyone that could reason would arm Negroes.

The papers carried the news that General Hooker had replaced General Burnside as commander of the forces opposing Lee. The rains in February and March reduced everything on that front to trying to survive. Men had a difficult time trying to get around in the mud and wagons and gun carriages promptly mired to the axle if they tried to move them.

April was still quite cold. This and the sharp increase in the price of everything caused by the decrease in the value of the Confederate money and the actual shortages, brought the bread riots in Richmond. It was touch and go with the rioters ready to take over the city until the combined appearance of the Virginia governor and Jeff Davis stalled their efforts. Davis made a strong appeal for reason and emptied his pockets as he flung his money to the crowd.

Tom found out from his sources that Davis had to make a trip to Arkansas to try to get help for the Vicksburg battle. No one not in the know of the independent reaction of governors and generals would believe the President of a new nation would not be able to order troops where they were needed. The states would agree the defense of Vicksburg was important to the future of their nation but would not agree to let 45,000 troops in camp in Arkansas be moved out of the state. The real refusal came from the general commanding this army who refused a direct appeal from President Davis. Most people thought the leaders in Richmond were so occupied with defense of Richmond that they did not recognize the fall of Vicksburg would be a major victory for the Federals. Davis and his staff did not try to refute the impression because it maybe was better to have people think you were dumb instead of knowing you could not get compliance with a logical request.

On April 22, they learned five gunboats had slipped past the batteries at Vicksburg, followed by more gunboats and troop transports on May 1. Grant at long last was making his move. On May 4 the papers carried the news Hooker was making his move to flank Lee. The next day they heard about the band of cavalry lead by General Stoneman. It was raging between Lee and Richmond; they got within two miles of the city. The same day they heard that Stonewall Jackson had been wounded but it was not until the seventh that they got the news about the battle of Chancellorsville.

Daniel and Tom knew young Dan had to be in the middle of this as he was a part of Stonewall's group but they did not say anything about it in front of Martha because they did not want her to worry. She recognized what they were doing and did not let them know she realized that they were trying in their way to protect her.

Jackson's left arm was amputated on May 7 and they and the rest of the country were shocked to learn Jackson died on May 11. Tom learned from his friends what had happened. Jackson had persuaded the medical staff to let his orderly attend him and when they were alone, Jackson had the orderly wet a blanket and place it upon him to cool his fever. He died from pneumonia instead of from his wounds.

The rout of Hooker at Chancellorsville was soon offset by the news Grant had crossed the Mississippi and was attacking the Confederate forces. When General Pembertson withdrew to Vicksburg, Tom thought, we have lost the day because he did not believe a relief column would be mounted. There was more and more talk that Pembertson was really a Yankee and that accounted for his willingness to trap himself. More than a few people blamed Davis for putting such a weak sister in this key spot.

On May 24 the papers carried the story from the New York papers that General Rhodes' troops had captured Martinsburg.

Again, Daniel and Tom did not discuss this news item in front of Martha but all three realized young Dan was on his way north. They were amazed that they got their information from Richmond papers and these papers carried no real news except what the papers gleaned from New York papers. Tom thought maybe it was better that way when they ran a Richmond story Lee's army was on the move with strict instructions not to disturb people. Also, they were to buy all the supplies they were gathering from the area. Tom said not even the fellow who wrote the yarn believes it. They must be on their way to Pennsylvania because that is where Stuart made such a good haul last year on his raid.

On July 4, the papers carried a New York story that Meade replaced Hooker as commander of the Federal armies. Tom thought this may mean trouble for us as this guy is a fighter but what a hell of a time to change your commander. It is not a fair shake for Meade but no one ever promised that life would be fair.

On the eighth, there was an account about a terrible battle at Gettysburg; Meade was falling back; Lee in pursuit; Vicksburg is relieved; and Bragg is still falling back. Tom and Daniel agreed there was not much you could believe in these reports; we should put them aside until there are more reliable reports.

By the tenth, there were reports Lee was falling back; Meade was not; and the rumors Lee had captured an army of 40,000 Yankees was false. By the next day, there were confirmed reports Vicksburg had fallen on July 4. Soon there were solid-appearing reports that Lee was making an orderly retreat and he had left his dead and wounded on the battlefield at Gettysburg. By the July 17, there were confirmed stories Lee was back in Virginia.

Daniel suggested Tom go to Richmond or wherever he needed to go to find out what had happened and whether young Dan was safe. Tom returned in a few days with the information there had been a great battle over several days and Lee was back in Virginia. Young Dan had been wounded in the leg and captured by the Federals; they did not know where he was being held. They did not think his wound was life threatening.

The Gettysburg battle, Tom reported, started as one of those accidental things that often happen to armies. The Confederates were foraging over a relatively large area in Pennsylvania and Lee was in touch with all his units except Stuart. A part of Hill's army started to Gettysburg because they heard there was a supply of shoes available there. Hooker and then Meade had been moving to intercept Lee's forces but assuring also that they stayed between Lee and Washington. One of Meade's advance cavalry units intercepted General Heth's advance guard about three miles beyond Gettysburg. Hill pushed forward with his units and General Reynolds called up the Federal forces. Meade had picked another location as his choice to wage a major battle but decided they should make a stand at Gettysburg and if needed fall back to the other location. He had worked out a plan that would enable him to move his forces over various routes. When he heard from Reynolds, he started his forces to Gettysburg.

Lee was not at Gettysburg until the end of the first day's fighting, July 1. He had received a message that Hill was attacking a sizable force near Gettysburg and asking that reinforcements be brought up. Lee pushed ahead with Anderson's unit and sent word to the other scattered units, they were to come to Gettysburg. Some divisions got there before Lee and they helped drive the Federals back through the town. When Lee and Longstreet arrived they decided that the Federals had regrouped south of town in a good defensive position and it was better not to press. Lee was still not able to contact his cavalry arm and felt the resulting lack of information and the weariness of his men from the day's fighting and marching made for a rest. This also supplied the time needed to plan the next day's action.

Lee looked over the terrain and decided this was not what he would choose but since the enemy was here and a battle somewhere in the area was called for, the earlier they got at it the better. He outlined his plan and got agreement from all except Longstreet who thought another plan would be better. Lee overruled and scheduled the attack on July 2 at the earliest hour that Longstreet could get his troops positioned to lead the attack. Lee thought that the earliest attack would be to his advantage because this gave the Federals less time to get their troops and supplies up and to prepare breast works. Lee did not consider withdrawing because the Potomac was at flood stage and he would face a delay in crossing which would expose his forces to much hazard. He arrived at the location where he should see Longstreet's forces go into action and found they had not arrived. He waited and waited and despite everything Lee could do, it was 4 P.M. before Longstreet began his attack and some support charges did not get into action until dusk. The fighting on Thursday, while a fierce fight, was too late and not coordinated. Lee did get his wandering cavalry back in his contact, although Stuart's men and mounts were exhausted from the long route they had been forced to take by Meade's troop deployment. The delay played into Meade's hand since he had more time to prepare defensive positions and to create reserves of men and material.

Friday's attack was planned that morning at a conference opposite Round Top. The attack was to start with an artillery barrage and then an assault led by General Pickett. Again, everyone was in agreement except Longstreet who thought the Federal artillery on Round Top would endanger his troops. Again, he was overruled and told to move in Pickett's support. About noon the attack opened with a massive artillery duel that lasted more than an hour. Before the Confederate's guns had finished their firings, the Federals were instructed to hold their fire; they wanted to conserve their ammunition for the rebel charge. The silence as the barrage was stopped produced an eerie sensation as Pickett's unit moved into their attack formation. Both the Federal musket and artillery fire were delayed until their effect would be better enhanced. Their fire, when it began, was severe; this action alone lost 4,000 men and Longstreet, again, was so late in getting into the fight that the results were all in favor of Meade's forces.

Lee withdrew his army to their prepared defensive positions. They rested and prepared for their retreat on the July 4 and it was evident by evening that Meade was not going to launch a counter attack. That night the Army of Northern Virginia began its long march back to Virginia. They could not remain where they were for fear their lines of supply and communication would be cut. They were prepared for trouble as they marched to the Potomac and they knew they would be tested somewhere on the route.

Tom's best information showed the battle caused 54,000 casualties including 25 generals and one son.

CHAPTER IX

Home

DAN was carried down the hill on a wheelbarrow and lifted onto some clean straw in a barn. The woman who had organized the parties to go up the hill looking for the wounded brought in a bucket of warm water and some clean rags. Dan thought nothing could feel better than the warm wet rag getting his face and hands clean again. She cleaned his wound as best she could without removing the splints Dan had made from the saber. Later in the day she was back with water, real coffee, and the most delicious potato soup that Dan could remember having. By nightfall that barn and every other barn, church and school had been filled with wounded Confederates and Federals. He was surprised the town people did not try to separate them by armies but they were busy tending to the wounded without difference to whether they were Confederates or Federals. The wounded were so thankful to see real human beings they did not care where they were while they continued to get the kind words, the hot food, the good coffee and good clean drinking water.

When Dan had been in the barn a week, he began to think about how he could make his way back to Virginia. He was not going to be able to walk, even if he could find or make a crutch. He wondered what the chances were of locating a gentle horse he could ride back. He would have to travel at night and avoid contact with people because no one but a wounded rebel would be trying to get back south. Then he remembered hearing about the hundreds of mules and horses they had "bought" before the battle and sent back to Virginia. A mount might be hard to find. He would have to work out a way get over the countryside and slip through the Yankee lines. He did not see an answer but he would keep trying to devise a plan. At least, he was being well treated by the townspeople and he was improving every day which was better than some poor souls were doing.

On Thursday, the July 16, new faces appeared and his lifestyle was suddenly changed. The Federal Provost Marshal appeared and took charge of the wounded. The first thing he did was to have the prisoners moved to a single location. No longer were they treated the same as the Federal wounded. The next cut was to segregate the prisoners into two groups; one that appeared to be close to death and the other group that might survive long enough to be transported for detention. Dan was in this latter group and on Friday, July 18 he found out what New York City looked like from David's Island. It looked like the Yankees had picked out an escape-proof island prison. They did get some shelter, some food and water and an occasional check by a doctor. By September he had been able to scramble for crude crutches and could get himself about in a fashion, although it looked like his wound was not healing. The leg seemed to be getting stronger each day; the break was healing but not the flesh wound. Shortly after they got to David's Island, they heard about the fall of Vicksburg on the first day he lay on Culp's Hill. They could not believe this key location had been allowed to fall but inquiry convinced them, it was fact not rumor. Some suggested Pemberton was really a yankee and maybe that accounted for him selling out as he did.

In the first few days of September, Dan found he was being segregated with others and then loaded aboard a ship. On September 8, Tuesday, he was one of several hundred who were being exchanged at City Point, near Richmond. He was surprised to see the Federals were so close to Richmond and was amazed at what he saw in Federal material along the river as contrasted with the worn condition of everything he saw when he got to Richmond. The Confederate doctors checked him and decided he should be sent to the hospital at Farmville. He caught the train to Farmville on Saturday, September 12.

When Dan reached the station in Richmond, he saw a company of Virginia infantry was boarding the same train. They helped him on the coach and asked him to ride in their coach with them. They wanted to know where he got his wound and when he told them Gettysburg, he opened a floodgate of questions. They had been left to guard Richmond when the army moved out and it was their first chance to talk to someone who had been through the campaign. Dan told them all that he knew about the movement into Pennsylvania and how pretty the farms looked. He skipped over the trauma he had when he heard the army move out without him and then finding the Federals had retired as well. They were amazed he thought he had received good care at David's Island. Time slipped by as they compared their experiences and the next thing Dan knew he was beyond Burkeville Junction where he should have changed cars.

Dan thought, I don't know how I did that but I would fancy going to Green Bay anyway. The boys in the Virginia company kidded him about the fact they had found their first deserter. Then they told him their current mission was to round up deserters in the northwestern part of North Carolina. Dan wanted to know why they needed a company to round up a few miserable ones. They informed him these few miserable ones had an established camp and had beaten off the local sheriff and the state militia Governor Vance had sent out to get them. They were instructed to bring them back dead or alive. They expected several would be brought in dead and others would be executed after they were tried. They told Dan they knew about several soldiers who had been executed after the troops got back from Pennsylvania. They were people who had been stragglers on the march north and had delayed rejoining their companies after Lee had returned to Virginia. Dan said he knew what Lee thought about soldiers who could not stay with the demands made on them. Dan said, "I know we have a problem but I don't think shooting our own men is right. Last year when General Jackson was ordered to have a soldier shot on the march into Maryland because he stole a pig, he moved the man into the most exposed position he had with instructions he was to be shot if he withdrew. He turned into a first class fighting man. It seems to me something like that is better than killing our own." The company though he had a point. Apparently, the current policy Davis had approved was for them to make an example of people who deserted or disobeyed orders. Dan said, "You are looking at one," and they had a good laugh.

They wanted to know how he would get to his home when they arrived in Green Bay. Dan said someone in the town would take him out or maybe someone from the family would be in town to pick up supplies. He thought his grandfather usually went into town each day to get the papers and to hear the current scuttlebutt. The agent at the station was a good friend of their family and his Grandfather Johns had helped him when his wife died. If nothing else, he could stay with the agent until someone came in to get him.

The soldiers helped him off the train as they got to Green Bay and as he hobbled around the station on his crutches, there was Macon in a wagon. The two could not have been more startled or happy to see each other. Macon jumped down and they greeted each other in a chorus of questions, trying to catch up with two years' experiences in the first few seconds.

Macon said, "Let me get your luggage."

Dan said, "This is it. You don't get much luggage in this man's army and even less as a prisoner of the Yankees."

Macon said, "Let me help you up the ramp to the freight platform and I will bring the wagon alongside. That will help get you aboard. Your grandfather is usually here but he thought I should bring the wagon in today since we had these supplies to bring out. I'll get the paper and be right back. Your grandfather'll be glad because they got him the sack of coffee beans he had ordered and now when he sees you, he'll think this is a blessed day."

Dan looked at the familiar sights as they rode out to the Johns house. It didn't seem like more than two years since he and Macon had ridden Maude and Dolly through here and in other ways it seemed like it was a long time ago.

Strange, he thought, I remember the odd crosscurrents I had when we rode out that day. I'm sure it will take some time to get used to doing what I want to do instead of what I'm told to do but I equally am sure I'll enjoy making the adjustment.

As they were entering the Johns' yard, Dan gave his three whistle signal he always used to tell his grandfather he was coming in. Daniel Johns nearly tore the hinges off the door getting out to see his namesake. He yelled to Eva. Eva, the cook, old Sam, and all the rest of the Negroes in the area rushed to see the returning soldier. They got into the wagon and helped lower Dan to the ground and then Macon and Sam grabbed each other's wrists to make a carry for Dan. They carried him into the house and eased him into a chair. Eva carried his crutches and got a pillow to put on a footstool to prop up his leg.

"Why didn't you let us know that you were coming?"

"Not supposed to be here. I missed my connection at Burkeville and came on here. I was exchanged at City Point on Tuesday and they have been keeping me busy ever since. I'm supposed to be in the hospital at Farmville for treatment on my leg and thought I would let you know where I was when I got there. It sure feels good to be here. Maybe, we can talk them into letting me recuperate here. I don't think there is anything much to do now but give the leg time to heal."

Daniel turned to Eva and told her to have Sam take the runabout to the Wootton's and tell them what had happened. "I know Martha will want to come right over and Tom can follow when he gets ready. Cook, get plenty of hot water and young Dan can have a bath and get the train dust off him. We could both use some good hot coffee."

Eva returned saying that Sam would be on his way shortly and was there anything they wanted.

Daniel Johns said, "We'll do fine with the coffee and the hot water the cook is bringing."

"Are you hungry?" asked Eva.

"Not now. The people on the train gave me some of their food but I would sure like to have some fried chicken for supper. You cannot imagine how often I have dreamed about how good it would be to get food like that again."

"That is easy to do. I'll tell the cook."

"You don't know how good it is to see you, Grandpa. There have been times I thought I never would see you again."

"No one has worried more about that than we have Dan. I'm sure it has been rough for you. How did you get your wound?"

"I got hit by a minie ball on the last day at Gettysburg on top of Culp's Hill. We almost had carried the hill when they got reinforced and forced us back. I tried to get behind a boulder and got my leg broken as the ball hit. There is some damage to the muscle that doesn't seem to be healing right."

"Eva, we could use some more coffee and my guess is that Martha and Tom will stay for supper."

"We'll take care of them. The bath is ready; should I have Macon help you get to your room?"

"Thanks, Eva. I can manage with my crutches. It just takes more time than I like.

"Grandpa, do you have something I can wear? I got this uniform issued after I got to Richmond and I have had to live in it ever since as this is the only thing I have. I will get a new issue of uniforms as I return to service. The agreement North Carolina has with the central government is the state will supply the uniforms and the central government will pay wages. At the moment, neither one is doing too good about either pay or uniforms but they both have promised to get even with me when I report back for service."

"I'm sure we can keep you decent, Dan. Eva will take your things and see they get cleaned and you can have anything that I have in the chest. I think you have grown since we were together and now we are closer to the same size. We are about the same height but you do not have as big a neck and chest as I do but you will get there, eventually. Do you need help getting your clothes off or getting into the tub? No, well I'll go get you some clothes and be back in a minute."

Young Dan slid into the tub of warm water and thought, "I can remember fussing about mom making me do this and now I think how lucky I am, again, to really relax and get clean."

Daniel came back in with some clothes saying, "Here are some clothes. They are a little snug for me but probably still will be too large for you. At least they are clean and they will keep you covered. I don't think you care about going dancing tonight anyway."

"Thanks, Grandpa. I'm sure they'll be just fine. Do you remember when I was around four or five and Mom would let me stay overnight here with you? I can remember on those cold winter nights how Eva or you would wrap a hot stove lid in towels or paper and put it in bed to keep my feet warm. There were so many covers on the bed that it felt like I couldn't turn over. I feel the same somewhat comfortable wonderful sensation now as I did then. Life would be great if we could stop it and enjoy those wonderful times. Then, I couldn't wait until morning because you were going to show me how to do something."

"Well, don't remember too long because your mother will be here shortly and she will come in whether you are in the all-together or not. Sure, I remember those days and the great times we had exploring our world. Yes, it would be great in some ways if we could hold onto a precious moment but we cannot stop the march of time and maybe would not want to if we could. If life was always that sweet and pleasant, for one thing, we wouldn't know how different it could be and we might get bored with it. The best we can do is to freeze those things in our memory and then we can bring them back and think about how good things were. You are thinner than I ever remember you being unless it was when you were three or four years old. I hope we can help put some meat back on those bones."

"If I had been fat, those Generals Jackson and Lee would have walked it off me and if they didn't get the fat off us, the food the Yankees have been giving us was never meant to do more than keep us alive. Although, I have to say the treatment we had at David's Island was fair. It was a long way from the food I'll get tonight and the last time when I slept in a bed like I will tonight, was when I stayed at Aunt Ethel's house in Richmond over two years ago. How is she? Have you heard from her? She was very good to me when I saw her."

"She died, Dan. Last winter was terrible cold as you know and she caught pneumonia and died. You probably don't know young Tom was killed at Sharpsburg."

"Poor Dad. That must have hurt him as much as it did for you to lose you sister. I was at Sharpsburg; that was a bloody battle for both sides. When we got to Frederick, Lee had a proclamation read to the citizens that we were there as their friends to help them. It would have done more good for me to read it to Maude and Dolly; at least they recognize me as someone that sometimes has an apple or a sugar cube for them. A bunch of uninvited strangers in your town overwhelming everything around and are obviously willing to fight, could never be considered friends. I don't know who suggested that to Lee but I bet he's been hiding ever since unless it could have been Davis. I'm sure sorry to hear about both Tom and Aunt Ethel; she was a good lady."

"She sure was. Tom's wife has gone back to her folks. Those

clothes are a little big but they do a job for you. Do you think you have to report to Farmville?"

"They will want to know where I am and will want to see me at some time but my guess is they have more patients than they can take care of now. I would like to be here if they have no rules forbidding it. I'll talk to Dad about it and see what he thinks. How are you two doing?"

"Better than I ever thought we would. Some good things happen in wartime you know; not much or many, but some."

Martha broke into the room and smothered Dan with hugs and kisses. "Oh Dan, you don't know how I have prayed for you to get back to us. Are you hurt bad?"

"Not as bad as many of my friends. I can't march and have a little discomfort but it's not bad. The main thing is I'm home and still have my leg. The break is healing nicely and maybe the wound will start to heal now."

"That surely isn't your uniform."

"Eva has my uniform, such as it is. These are Grandpa's clothes. I'll get my regular uniform issued when I go back for duty."

Tom came in and they went over much the same ground.

Dan said, "I'm sorry to hear about losing young Tom. We were in the same battle but we never saw each other. We may not have been in the same area of Maryland until the battle gathered at Sharpsburg. We had been at Boonsboro until we pulled back."

Eva announced cook had supper ready if they wanted to eat now. Dan thought he had never eaten anything that tasted better. To sit down with your family and have good food like this, must be one of life's simple but warmer experiences. When he started supper, he thought there will never be enough but his hunger soon turned into I-wish-I-could-but-I-can-not eat more.

With supper finished and enjoying the last cup of good coffee, Tom asked if he felt like going over his experiences on the Pennsylvania campaign. Dan told them what he had done on the campaign and how close they came to succeeding on July 3 and briefed them on the time he spent alone on the battlefield. He did not feel that he wanted to re-live the despair he felt as they abandoned him and hundreds of others. A frank portrayal would force him to do it. Dan asked his father what he thought about reporting to Farmville and Tom said he was going to Farmville on Monday on some other business. It would be no trouble to stop by and discuss the matter with the officer in charge. He did not think there would be any further requirement. Dan relayed the discussion he had with the Virginia company on the way out and found they knew about the people in northwest North Carolina. His father thought they were a sorrier lot than the people of what was now called West Virginia.

They all met at the Wootton household for Sunday dinner and Dan got to renew acquaintances with his sister and his two younger brothers. This began a series of pleasant days with his family. Tom returned on Wednesday with the word Dan could stay where he was until he had recovered and then they would want to see him. The days and the weeks drifted by in pleasant food and company. Dan was surprised at the pleasure he now got in some things he used to take for granted; like having a bed to sleep in, or a room to himself, or having regular meals.

Dan was surprised to learn their paper still carried stories from the North. He was amazed they had gotten the report of the New York City riots that happened about the time he got to David's Island. They had to laugh at the report on October 7 that a chief of the medical department in Washington had been discharged for passing the information to a reporter about the 54,000 Federal losses in the Gettysburg campaign. They got the report on October 28 that Grant was now in charge. None of them thought this was good news for the South.

Each day Eva bathed his wound which was just below the knee and applied some salve she made from native herbs. She used clean rags each day for washing and for the bandages. The used materials were boiled before they were allowed back in the house. Day by day, they could see the proud flesh decrease which showed the healing was progressing satisfactorily. It was just going to take time to get full control back and it might never really be normal but it should progress enough to give him adequate support. As the healing progressed, Eva massaged the lower leg and foot to try to improve the circulation.

In early December, they heard Davis had at long last removed General Bragg, his friend, from command. Everyone, other than Davis, thought the move had been long overdue and thought Davis was endangering his own ability to effectively lead by continuing to support his friend. Bragg clearly had shown he could not handle a major assignment. Shortly after they heard about this move, they learned Bragg's new assignment was in Richmond as Davis' principal advisor on military affairs. This placed him in a prime position to do much mischief and always lay the blame on someone else. There was a great outcry against Davis this time. He had effectively taken the heat off General Bragg and placed it on his own shoulders.

Most people thought they would be lucky if they could somehow create a situation for peace to be negotiated. Some thought they had effectively lost the war and a peace try should be made without destroying more of our seed corn in the loss of life and capital. If we wait until after the 1864 elections, we would probably find the Federal positions had firmed. Davis chose to dream the peace party might carry the fall elections in the north.

This Christmas of 1863 was the happiest the Johns and the Wootton households had experienced in some years. They had their first-born back and he might not be with them much longer but the war was teaching everyone to take things as you found them today.

The war outlook was not good but they hoped Lee could get some sense into things. As people lost confidence in Davis' ability, they transferred their loyalties to General Lee. They did not know Lee was pressing Davis for food often getting down to next day's supply before he got any action. He was as persistent in trying to get more men into service. The first outward proof of this was the outcry from the railroads and the governors. They insisted they had to retain their employees as exempt from the draft and Lee thought they should all be sent into service. They could take battle casualties who could not march to do their jobs. Lee and Davis were considering how they could integrate Negroes into the service since this was the largest untapped manpower pool they had. It was an explosive issue with violent reactions every time the Confederate soldier saw the Negro in a Yankee uniform. It would take some doing to get him to agree they could wear the Confederate uniform.

In the middle of February, Dan felt that he was recovering enough that he might be able to do light duty. He and his father took the buggy to Farmville and Dan was checked by the doctors there on the sixteenth. They gave him a sixty-day furlough; he was to report back to his unit on the seventeenth of April. He hated to leave the family nest that had been so pleasant for the last six months. There had not been much marching and fighting by his unit during the winter months but he knew things would pick up as the weather warmed and the roads improved.

CHAPTER X

Cotton Trade

DAN and his father returned home from Farmville with the news he was due back with his company by the middle of April. They should make the most of the time they had left in getting things ready for the warrior to return to the army. He would need clothing and it was unlikely North Carolina would be able to supply what was needed. Governor Vance was appealing to the people of the state to take up their rugs to be made into coats or blankets for the soldiers. Shoes and boots had been a supply problem for some time and it did not appear they were going to get what was needed. Between the Wootton and Johns households, they could see young Dan started off with enough to keep him covered and well shod. For many Confederate soldiers, their families were in no position to help the soldier members. Many desertions could be laid to the distress the soldiers' families were having in trying to get enough to eat.

By the end of February, a colonel who was an old time friend of Tom's showed up at the Wootton home. After a short visit, Tom brought him to the Daniel Johns' home with the information that they could trust the Colonel. He had a mission he wanted young Dan to do; it would need the utmost care and secrecy. It would involve Daniel Johns as well. The Colonel told Daniel and young

Dan what they already knew; there was a serious shortage of many things and the most critical was the supply of medicines. The Colonel had found he could arrange a trade with a northern agent. The traffic was known by people on both sides but it was not discussed and was not to include war materials. The Confederate command thought young Dan should accept this extra duty. There might be some danger and some discomfort involved but the medical staff really needed the supplies to be secured by trading with these agents. The materials we have been able to get through the blockade runners have never been enough and the source was rapidly disappearing.

Young Dan said he was willing to try but he didn't understand how he could arrange this trade. The Colonel said, "I'll make the arrangements and you'll have to do the part of getting the material to the site and bringing back the supplies. The exchange of cotton is for medical supplies and we will expect you and one of your grandfather's slaves to drive the wagons to the exchange site and to return with the supplies. We will allow your grandfather to ship a few bales for exchanges he may want because we will be asking him to help get the wagons in repair and the horses in shape for the trip. It will involve traveling by back roads and avoiding discussing your mission with the nosy people you may meet. It's still winter and you may have some nasty weather on the trip."

Young Dan said, "I should be able to handle that; when do you want me to start?"

The Colonel said, "I'll contact the agent and come back to give you the details. It will involve your taking the wagons to a location near the border with what the Yankees now call West Virginia and returning through here and then to Richmond, Mr. Johns," the Colonel said, "I'll try to get as good equipment as I can find, but you'll have to check it over and verify it can make the trip, even if you have to use your own wagons, gear or horses. I can allow you to include five bales. You will have to supply the forage for the trip to the border and for the trip from here to Richmond and the supplies your people will need for the trip. The horses that I can supply may not be what either of us would like but they may be able to do the work if you can feed them grain for the few days they will rest here and supply grain for them on the trip. They have not been used to good forage because we just do not have it but they often make amazing recovery when they are given good food and adequate treatment."

Daniel Johns asked if he could get green coffee and salt and if possible he would like some exchange to be made in gold.

The Colonel thought the arrangement could be made. "If we're in agreement, I'll make the contacts and arrange the details and be back when I have more information. I think I could be back by the middle of March."

The Colonel was back on the seventeenth of March and only stayed long enough to relay the information that he would try to have the wagons at the Johns' farm on the twenty-fifth of March. Young Dan should try to leave on the thirtieth of March. The wagons would be left at the farm early in the morning and no one on the farm should try to speak to the teamsters or to have any contact with them. If it was successful, the farm would find two wagons near the barn and not know how they got there. The Colonel would not be seen again, but would have occasional surveillance made to see things were going all right. Young Dan would find there were guns and ammunition on board for his use but he should avoid an armed exchange if possible. He should try to be on the road south of Bedford, Virginia on Sunday, April 3. He should find two wagons near the road; he was to tie his teams to the fence and get aboard the other wagons and return. He should not see anyone and should not try to find anyone. The wagons would appear to be loaded with forage and he should make no attempt to verify the load until they arrived back at his grandfather's. The Colonel said, "If there are no questions, I'll be shoving off. I have been away from Richmond too long as it is."

Shortly after the Colonel left the weather started to change. By

Sunday it was very cold, colder than it had been at anytime during the winter. It not only stayed cold; it started to snow on Tuesday, March 22 and continued on past Wednesday. It was the heaviest snow that they had seen for several years. Daniel Johns thought, "They'll never get those wagons here on time if they're having to travel in this weather."

But, on Friday, March 25, Daniel Johns heard the two wagons pull into the farm yard before daylight and before Eva came in with his morning cup of coffee. He thought he could hear the two drivers leave on horseback and assumed they had brought their mounts with them.

When there was good daylight, Daniel Johns went out to see what he had been left and to see what repairs were needed. He could tell by the sound they made in bringing the wagons into the yard he must have all the wheels pulled and the axles greased. Otherwise, the wagons seemed to be in good repair except for one wheel that might need a new spoke. The horses could use a good feeding and some harness might have to be mended or replaced. He got Sam to take over the direction of the needed work and returned to the house for coffee and his usual breakfast. Eva wanted to know if she should wake young Dan.

Daniel said, "Let him sleep. He'll have to do without a good bed and enough sleep soon enough. There is nothing he can do about the wagons now. The work to be done already is started."

Sam and his crew got the wagon wheels off the ground one at a time by using a fulcrum and a four-by-four as a lever. They greased the axles and tightened the wheel bolts. Sam found one of the wheels did need a spoke replaced and all the brake shoes should be re-blocked. He took the wheel to the blacksmith shop and got the carpenter started on replacing the brake blocks. He got one of the boys to oil the horse collars and look for signs of extra wear. One of the horses had already lost a shoe and most of them could do with new shoes. He found one line was frayed and should be replaced and some harness would have to be replaced.

When young Dan awoke, he was surprised to learn the wagons had arrived and the corrective work was proceeding. When he finished his breakfast, he went out to see what he had in store for the trip. The first thing he found was the Colonel had arranged for him to have two of the new repeating carbines they had apparently taken from Yankee dead, wounded or prisoners. There was nothing made like it in the Confederacy and Dan had never seen one but had heard about the firepower that could be generated with these ten shot rifles. They were so new only special units of the Federal forces had them. They probably came from the cavalry raids the Yankees were now using more and more. Daniel Johns had never seen them.

The work on making ready for the trip proceeded day by day. Young Dan found some singletrees did not look too strong and traded them for the Johns variety. They also found one of the king pins showed wear and had the blacksmith make a new one. The kerosene lanterns the men had used on the wagon tongues to get to the farm at night might prove to be useful on their trip, though they did not plan to travel at night. The main use might be to let them travel until dark instead of stopping early enough to make camp.

They were busy but by the twenty-ninth, they agreed they could start the next morning. On Wednesday, March 30, they started soon after daylight on the road to Farmville. Daniel Johns on his saddle mare rode with them and as they neared the Wootton house, there were Tom and Martha in the buggy ready to travel with them for the first few hours. The dinner stop was like a picnic. Kitty had prepared a feast for them and young Dan was sure this meal would be one of the trip's highlights. Somehow it seemed easier to part after the noon break and the splendid food than it would to have said goodbye as they left the farm. Tom and Daniel were satisfied the boys and the equipment were in good shape to make the trip. Partings are never easy thought Dan but this is better than most for I soon should be seeing them and will have added something for their welfare and for the cause.

Dan and Macon turned off before they got to Farmville and made camp for the night. They camped the next night near the village of Red House, then near Rustbury and on Saturday, April 2, they were beyond Evingston. As they made camp that night, Dan told Macon they should find the wagons they were going to take back along side the road south of Bedford tomorrow. Macon wanted to know how they would know. "Would there be people there to take their wagons?"

Dan said, "We'll tie our teams to the rail fence or tree and then we'll take our gear as quickly as we can and leave on the other wagons. I'll know we have the right wagons and we do not want to see or talk to anybody."

Macon said, "It seems awful funny to me; how do we know the right person will take our wagons?"

Dan said, "It's funny business all right but it's important we do as we were instructed. There probably is someone watching us make the swap and they'll come out and take our wagons when we get out of sight."

By mid-morning, Dan could see there were two wagons and teams standing by the side of the road ahead of them. He drove his team to the opposite side of the road, tied them to the small tree nearby and started back the way they came when Macon had transferred their gear. He had an uneasy feeling he was being watched but he could not see anyone and did not stop until a late hour for their dinner break, so they would be out of sight if there had been someone hiding near the exchange location.

They had an uneventful trip back to the farm at Green Bay and arrived there on Thursday afternoon, April 7. There was much rejoicing in the Wootton and the Johns households that the two young bucks had finished this part of their mission. Daniel Johns was happy he had a supply of salt and coffee and a small amount of gold. All three commodities were becoming hard to come by as the Confederate currency declined in value and the Yankee navy increased its stranglehold on the Confederate ports. When the Confederate government refused to accept their own paper money as payment for taxes, the decline in value of the Confederate currency became very steep.

Young Dan and Macon enjoyed three days rest and family care, while Daniel Johns and Sam checked the teams, the gear and the wagons to see that everything was ready for the trip to Richmond. They made ponchos for the two young bucks because spring had begun in earnest and it looked as if it might continue to rain. Daniel Johns was thankful they would have good roads on the way in and should not have a problem with stream crossings.

Young Dan and Macon got started on the road to Richmond on Monday morning, April 11. The weather broke for them in the morning but it looked like it would rain before night. The Richmond papers had been carrying reports from Washington and from New York about Grant planning and preparing for an assault on Richmond. Everyone assumed this march would not begin until the weather cleared and the streams had returned to their normal levels. If he intended to get to Richmond, he would need dry ground to be able to get his supplies moved. Everyone, they were sure, could remember the trouble General Hooker got into trying to move his troops in the rainy season.

As they had when the two young bucks started to West Virginia with the cotton, the family group accompanied the two on the first leg of their journey. When they stopped for dinner the rains had returned and Daniel Johns was glad they had brought both buggies this time. He would have gotten damp if he had been riding his mare. This way, they could put up the curtains and stay warm and dry. They stretched a tarpaulin between trees and had an enjoyable dinner, despite the rain. As they parted, young Dan gave his grandfather one of the repeating carbines and a box of shells the Colonel had supplied. Maybe this would replace the good Spencer young Dan had left somewhere on the field at Gettysburg. Daniel Johns was overjoyed to get such a fine gun but was worried about what would happen to young Dan when he arrived in Richmond and he was missing one gun. Tom said he should not worry; the gun had not been signed for by Dan and they would be so glad to get the supplies they would not make a case about the gun. The goodbyes were made after dinner and the Woottons and Daniel Johns turned their buggies back to Green Bay and the two young bucks started to the town of Jennings Ordinary.

Young Dan and Macon made good progress in the afternoon and camped near Jennings Ordinary the first night out, made camp the second night near Jetersville, near Skinquarter the third night and on the Hull Street Road as they approached Richmond on the fourth night. They were making such good time, they would have a day or two before Dan was to report for service. They still had some of Eva's good food basket left and did not have to search for their sustenance. They felt they had been pretty lucky to have made the trip without having trouble with the horses or equipment. They had to admit the horses and the wagons they received in the trade were somewhat better than what they had left for the Yankees. Dan told Macon he should see the stock pile of material the Yankees had east of Petersburg.

Dan said, "When they brought us up the James River for the prisoner exchange at City Point, I could see the material they had. I'll guarantee you nothing in like amount is available for Lee's army. They have more soldiers than we do, they have more horses and mules, more food, and what is really beginning to hurt, is they have more and better guns than we have. This is especially true of our artillery. They sure out-gunned us at Gettysburg and they seem to get better each year in the use of their artillery and cavalry."

Macon said, "How're we going to know where we are supposed to take these wagons?"

Dan said, "Don't worry. There's been someone watching us for the last two days and maybe longer. I'm sure someone will come out and escort us to the place we are going before we need to worry about it."

As Hull St. Road was ready to take them into Richmond proper, they found the Colonel and a mounted squad waiting for them in a side street.

Dan saluted and the Colonel said, "I'm glad to see you made it in good time, young man. You must have had good luck all along the line to get here this early. Follow me and I'll show you where to park the wagons."

They followed the Colonel through Richmond and parked the wagons in the courtyard of the main hospital Dan had been in when he was exchanged. They took their gear from the wagons and the Colonel showed them where to wait while he went to see the medical officer. When he returned, he told Macon to stay with the gear, while he took Dan to the doctor. Dan thought he got a lot more attention than when he had been here before. The doctor finished his examination and was surprised the people at Farmville had sent him back for service when his leg had not healed. Dan could walk on it in a fashion but he would not be able to maintain a forced march pace. The doctor and the Colonel conferred in a corner of the room for a few minutes and then the Colonel said, "Come on with me, Dan."

When they got to the courtyard, the Colonel told one of the men in the squad to take Dan and Macon to his home. He told Dan to stay there until the Colonel could get back to him. He said, "My wife will have the cook fix you anything you want to eat and she'll find a place for your man. I expect to be home for supper and think I'll have your assignment worked out when I get there. You may be at my place for a day or two."

When the Colonel arrived home for supper, he brought the news Dan and Macon could both be used driving ambulances for Hood's army. He had telegraphed Daniel Johns and received his permission to keep Macon for some time. Though Dan could not march at the moment, he and Macon working together could load and unload the wounded and release two drivers who could be returned to the fighting service. Dan could stay as the Colonel's guest for Saturday and Sunday which would give him time to find out where they were to report.

CHAPTER XI

Elmira, New York

DAN found Hood's camp and got Macon and himself settled into their life as drivers on Monday, April 18. Contrasted to the life the regular soldier led in the army camp, they were living in the lap of luxury. They were warm and dry and got hot food for their meals and at the moment, they were not very busy. The two men they replaced were unhappy to be placed back in the regular service. Dan heard one of them had deserted the next day after being sent back to his unit. Desertion was becoming a not uncommon occurrence and was a source of concern to the officers about how they could stem this loss. Desertion was draining the ranks of effectives and the trials took time and executions were having a depressing effect on the troops. No one had a better answer than to try to speed up the trial process to assure the execution followed immediately after the deserter was captured.

Macon being used as an ambulance driver did not seem to stir any ire. The practice of using slaves for preparing defense positions had been used by both sides since early in the war. Some were used by the officer corp to improve the quality of camp life and there lately had been an effort to secure slaves for draymen. They had not been assigned to artillery units but the debate was beginning on how to tap this manpower source for the fighting units. Lee had observed this was the one remaining manpower source the South had not tapped and the Federals were making good use of the slaves in occupied territory or who had escaped into Federal hands. Everyone knew about Lincoln's proclamation and thought their slaves would not hear about it. They were mystified about how they got the information when they heard the subject being discussed by their slaves.

Lee thought the matter should be pursued though he saw there were severe political and emotional problems which had to be solved. He needed more soldiers and the enemy was tapping this source. Here was a manpower pool of some two million who could help preserve the Confederacy. There were important questions about how to treat slave soldiers to get them to accept a fighting role. To start, they would have to promise them their freedom once the war was won. This presented major problems about how to deal with the owner. Was the owner to be paid for his slave now, was the slave to remain his property until after the war, what should the black soldier be paid, who should get the pay were some questions for which there were no ready answers. The Negro troops would have to be kept in separate companies and under the command of white officers as the Federals were doing. The Federal black troops fought valiantly when they were properly trained and because they knew the Confederates would not take black prisoners. Would they fight as well for their Confederate officers or would they shoot their officers and surrender to the Federals? They were unhappy with the half pay the Federals were giving them and had not been able to get what they termed justice on other issues.

Most of the Southern command became choleric at the mention of the subject and they could not communicate their disgust. This was supposed to be a gentleman's war to make people let us alone, so we can continue our peculiar institutions and our life style. Some would wrestle with their emotions and set the problem aside to indulge in bourbon. Many could not face the reality that what they visualized had not existed for some time. It would never be even the same as it had been before the start of the war. The question now became one of how to survive and keep some direction of our lives or being defeated and having the heel of the hated abolitionists directing or misdirecting our lives and destroying our sacred structured illusion.

Dan and Macon led carefree lives for about two weeks. They had to make several trips each day to the front lines not to pick up battle casualties for the military action was quiet but to take the usual number of people wounded by their own carelessness. It seemed even at this late date people were still being injured by their own weapons and the lack of care in camp sanitation. The injuries which resulted in the amputation of arms or legs haunted Dan. He heard the screams while the work was being done and the agonizing cries as the bandages were being changed. Dan could not believe how lucky he had been to escape such treatment when he had been wounded at Gettysburg. His leg might not be as sound as he would like it to be but he felt lucky to have a leg instead of a stump.

As the month ended, they became busier than they thought possible. Grant's long-awaited campaign started to move through the wilderness area and the list of wounded looked like it would never end. The weather was generally good except occasional morning fogs made finding their way to the front and back to the base difficult. There was no assurance a road that had been secure a few hours ago would be safe on the return trip. Both sides were losing men and equipment by stumbling into each other's areas. The battle front seemed to be a blood bath without an actual victory for either side. The difference being this time, the Federals kept coming back day after day instead of pulling back. As Grant and Meade moved, they left fields soaked by blood from the dead and the wounded from both armies. Dan thought Antietam and Gettysburg had been bad affairs but no worse than what they were going through now.

They made so many trips they lost track of the number much less the wounded soldiers they took to the surgeons. They were on the go from the earliest ray of light until it was too dark to follow the road. They ate whenever they could get close enough to the mess tent to grab something, caught their teams by lantern light and unharnessed them and fed them by lantern light as they shut down for the day. Dan would wake up at night and believe he was still hearing the screams before he got awake enough to realize that he was having a nightmare.

The foggy mornings were special hazards for them. More than once, they had almost blundered into the Federal lines. The territory was difficult at best and you were never certain who might be in control. More than once Dan stopped the team and left Macon to keep them quiet and he walked ahead to scout whether they were coming up on a Federal camp or one of their own. In the heavy fog, you could get close to the pickets and listen to their speech to tell which side they were on. Pickets always seemed to talk more when it was foggy.

By the seventh of May, the action moved south and east to the Spottsylvania area. The field medical center moved south on the road to Richmond near Thromburg. Dan and Macon thought they would never see the end of torn bodies which streamed from the fighting. By everything they could learn, the Federal casualties were heavier than those of the Confederates but this did not seem to deter the Federal attack. On Monday, Dan got word his company commander wanted him to report back to his company. He gathered up his gear and rode most of the way back with Macon as he made another trip with the ambulance.

As they made their way to the front, Dan said, "You know we're losing this war and you have to decide what you want to do. You know you can escape to the Federal lines on any foggy morning and once there you'll have your freedom but maybe not what you would like it to be. If you decide to try it, I hope you don't join their fighting units for I wouldn't like to think I might have to kill you or that one of my friends would. The Federals will only pay you one half what they pay their white soldiers and you value your life as much as any man. I hear the Federals are trying to train the blacks at Sea Island and they have organized schools and camps there. If you try to get there, maybe you can learn some useful skill or trade. We're in for rough times as far as I can see. If you stay with what you are now doing, you have some small risk but nothing like what I'll be facing. You'll be free when the war is over but maybe you should think about getting a head start when you get a good opportunity. I don't want to know what you may decide but for old times' sake be cautious. There are mean people in this army and in the Federal army. But, there are some great people in the north and in the south. I think I'll always hate the Yankees as a group and I surely do not mind killing the bastards I face in combat. They're destroying our life and for that, I'll always hate them. On a one-to-one basis, there are some that can be decent. You'll find there are more people in the Federal army that hate blacks than there are people interested in your welfare. If that is the route you take, be cautious. You can let me off here. My company is just over the ridge from here. Hood's command is the road to your left."

Dan watched as Macon turned the team into the road leading to Hood's camp and as the ambulance started to disappear around a bend in the road, they exchanged their now familiar two-tone whistle. Dan thought even though he's a slave, he's a friend and we have had many good times together. I don't know if we'll ever see one another again. I'm sure he'll use the first opportunity to drive the ambulance into the Federal lines. I don't know how I could blame him. He has heard about all the great things that will happen to him once he is free and I can't blame him for grabbing the chance. I think he has enough native resources to survive, no matter what they throw his way.

Dan found his company had moved into the front lines and they were busy preparing a strong defensive position. They were assigned a spot in the center where there was a sharp angle in the line and used the quiet day to prepare formidable breastworks. If the enemy were to attack here, they would pay a very dear price for the try. On Tuesday, the tenth, a sharp attack was made on their left that almost broke through their lines. Only a last minute surge by the Texans saved the day. They learned the Federal cavalry had very nearly made it to Richmond before it was blocked by General Stuart. General Stuart had been killed in the raid and although the raid did not result in the capture of the Confederate capitol, it did deal a severe loss to the army of northern Virginia. Stuart would be as hard to replace as had been Jackson. The eleventh, Wednesday, was spent in bringing up supplies and preparing for the coming assault. Part of the Confederate strength was withdrawn late at night to prepare for an expected try to slide to the east. It had been assumed the withdrawal would be made without Grant knowing the center had been weakened. They turned in for the night on Wednesday feeling they had things about as safe as they could be made. What they did not know was the Federals had learned of the withdrawal and they had planned an attack for the early morning of the twelfth. As it happened, there was a dense fog in the early hours and the Federal attack was made quietly. They were completely surprised and overrun without a shot being fired. The Federals captured 3,000 men and two generals before the Confederates were aware of the attack.

Dan thought, "Here, I'm a prisoner again and I haven't fired a shot since Gettysburg."

They found the provost marshall was already here as contrasted with his late arrival at Gettysburg. They were moved to the rear into well-prepared positions. By Monday, the sixteenth, they were moved across the Potomac into Maryland to Point Lookout. They could be held here with a very small force. There were miles of water in three directions and little chance they could escape.

They soon settled into the camp routine. They were furnished tents and a blanket and were supplied with one hot meal a day.

Since most of the battalion in the line had been captured intact on the 12th, they knew their fellow prisoners and largely continued their structure and relationship as they had before capture. It was not living as they would have liked it but it was better than they had thought it would be.

Days to weeks and weeks to months with little or no change. They could see the Federal transports steaming past the point. They were pouring material and replacements in the fight for Richmond. Before the end of June, the Federals gathered the officers and took them to other locations. No reason was given but the camp assumed someone had overheard the officers planning an escape. By the end of July, the whole camp was aware of a plan being developed in Richmond to run a load of weapons into the shore at night and the camp could overpower the small guard unit. The plan was for them to capture enough material and supplies to march up the peninsula and threaten or take Washington. Dan and his buddies thought they had heard of crazy schemes before but not one that was any more cockeyed than this. In the first place, nothing like this could be discussed or planned in either Richmond or Washington without the other side hearing about it. They were sure the Federals had heard about the plan when the guards were increased and patrols were started in the offshore waters. This was followed by armed and detailed searches of their campgrounds. On the 10th of August, they were marched in small groups to a railhead where they were put on cars with armed guards and by the weekend they found themselves in the prisoner stockade near Elmira, New York. The stockade at Elmira had been finished in January, 1864 and Dan's group nearly finished filling the camp. They got their one meal a day which they learned to call bean soup because the usual fare was supposed to be a bean dish but always seemed to be watered down. The camp wit tried to make a joke of it by saying, "Here Ben, hold my hat, while I dive into this soup and see if there's a bean in it."

At this stockade there was little exchange between the prisoners and the guards due to the design of the stockade. Guards were placed on the perimeter of the stockade with a patrolling walk built into the walls about sixteen feet above ground level. The walls were two inch slabs usually three or four feet wide and buried four feet into the ground. The guards had a four-foot extension above the walkway which gave them a chance to move from one area to another in a crouch without being seen. They were on patrol around the clock and the interior of the camp was lighted by lamps that hung from brackets attached to the wall. Day or night the prisoners could be observed in the yard area by guards. The usual practice at night was for the guards to make enough noise on the walkway and in exchanges between the guards to remind the prisoners they were alert enough to prevent any escape try.

The prisoners were quartered in huts equipped with bunks or shelving around the perimeter of the room. Each man was given one blanket and as the nights began to get cold, they learned how to double-up by spreading one blanket on the boards and then use the other blanket for cover. When winter really arrived they found they could survive by sleeping four to a bunk with one blanket on the boards and the other three over them. It was a case of one turn, all turn but they could survive what to them was a bitter winter. They learned to maintain the camp's sanitation level and to get enough exercise with group sessions to maintain their muscle tone and some semblance of spirit. What they heard about the war's progress did little to cheer them up.

April arrived with little change in the routines; policing the grounds and exercise sessions each morning until the noon meal arrived. They did get good coffee which to most of them was a treat they would not have had in their trenches at Richmond. They did not believe the first reports Richmond had fallen; they assumed it was a Yankee trick. Later they heard about the surrender at Appomattox and then a few days later they were stunned to hear about the assassination of Lincoln. They worried they might be singled out for rough treatment, not because they in any way had anything to do with it but they were the enemy and nearby. The capture of Booth and the others seem to allay the tension they might be used.

The capture of Jefferson Davis in Georgia on May 10 seemed to them to end a long string of foolish actions. He apparently had not been able to understand what had happened much less to be able to foresee that it could happen. To try to run and hide did not make sense to soldiers; when you were beaten, the proper action was to surrender. Whatever bargaining rights he might have had for the South were destroyed by a dumb escape try that had no chance to succeed. He placed himself in position to be treated as a common crook instead of as a leader who had failed.

Dan and the rest of the camp were surprised and delighted in June as the Yankees began to process the prisoners for their return home. On Wednesday, the 21st, they put Dan on a train that took him to the docks at New York. He and his group were put on board a ship and they headed out of the harbor. They were not told where they were going but they guessed they would be disembarked somewhere close to their home destination. By the end of June, they were entering the harbor at Savannah. Dan figured it will be a long tough walk back to Virginia. The boat docked and they were told they were free to go; the Yankees had enough of them and they were not sorry to leave the Yankee presence. Dan thought I remember that Macon said once, "When you ain't got, you make do." And boy if there's ever a time for me to make do, it is now.

As Dan started to leave the dock area, wondering where he could find something to eat, he was startled to hear a whistle that sounded like the one he and Macon had used. It seemed long ago and Macon would not be here in Savannah. He looked around and did not see anyone he recognized. As he walked to the town center, he heard the two-note whistle again.

CHAPTER XII

Macon

MACON thought about what young Dan had told him and the more he thought about it, the more he wanted to make a break for the Federal lines the first time he got a good chance. Meanwhile, he would try to assemble things he might need when he did make the break. He needed a light pack with enough things to allow him to live off the land until he could reach a point of safety and where he could be able to choose his own options. He had the beginnings of what he needed in his tarpaulin and blanket. He needed some food and matches and if possible a knife. He would watch his chances and see what he could get as the opportunities presented themselves. There were some catch-as-catch-can instances as the wounded were loaded into the ambulance and he would make the most of whatever came his way.

The weather got misty and foggy in the next week and by then Macon had accumulated some hardtack and had found some matches and a knife, courtesy of some wounded who probably would never miss the loss. The armies were moving to the east and south which left the usual amount of confusion if the Confederates should catch him before he got to the Federal lines. He took the turn for the Federal lines on his first morning trip. When he thought he had gone far enough to be even or behind the Federal lines he turned west and then north to try to get clear of any contact with troops, either Federal or Confederate. When the day cleared enough to see any distance, Macon pulled the ambulance into the protection of a creek bank and let the horses have a drink. He took his tarpaulin and found himself a spot some distance from the ambulance; he did not want not to be trapped if someone rode by.

He could hear the artillery to the south and east of his location and he thought, "I'll head further north before I turn east. I'd like to get within striking distance of the coast and see if I can find a Negro group somewhere in the area. They should know more than I do what would be the right thing for me to do. I don't want any part of the armies on either side. I need to try to get something to do either to live here or to work my way down to Sea Island."

Macon followed a northern track for another hour. He could see the terrain was becoming more open and he decided he had pressed his luck as far as he dared. It was better to abandon the ambulance and the team than to run the risk of being stopped and taken to an army center for questioning. He unhooked the team and turned them loose. He would have ridden one of the horses but he thought the risk of the extra attention made walking the thing to do. He turned east and tried to keep as close to cover as he could. If someone came along, he could take cover and see if he thought it would make a safe contact.

Macon traveled for two days, keeping out of sight when he heard or saw someone. He crossed a busy railroad by waiting until nightfall. He stayed alongside a creek that gave him water and cover. His supply of hardtack was sustaining him but he wished he dared to light a fire and have something hot. By mid-morning on the third day, he came to the largest body of water he had ever seen. He thought he had made it to the ocean but then he saw there was land across the way; it must be a bay or the biggest river he had ever seen. He looked up and down the banks and all he could see was one black man in a boat about half a mile below him.

He seemed to be fishing. Macon kept under cover and worked his way down to where the man was fishing. He would move the boat along the shoreline and every now and then would haul a funny looking flat fish into the boat. As far as Macon could tell, the fisherman did not know Macon was watching from the brush that concealed him. The man had white hair but seemed to be able to move swiftly and with grace when he spotted the fish he wanted. Macon thought Master Dan and he had fished but we never fished with a spear nor did we ever catch a fish that was flat. Macon was ready to step out of his hiding place and hail the man when he saw a steamboat was coming down the channel or river. He thought I better not show myself until there is no one around except the two of us. The first boat was followed by several others and Macon could spot more smoke on the horizon. He stayed in place but the thought about how good the fish would taste almost made him cry.

By mid-afternoon, the traffic disappeared and as he thought now is the time to move out and hail the man, he saw the fisherman was rigging a small sail. He tacked in quite close to where Macon was hiding and called:

"Hey, you in there. If you need help come on out."

Macon was astonished. He was sure no one could have spotted his approach; he looked around to see if there was someone else the fisherman was hailing. He moved out of his hiding place and asked, "How'd you know I was there."

The man said, "I've been watching you ever since you hit the shoreline and the birds would give you away if I hadn't seen you go into hiding."

Macon thought I heard those birds but I was so interested in the new things I was seeing I forgot they were giving a signal. Macon pulled himself and his gear from the hiding place and walked to the waters edge. He said, "I came through the battle lines or around them and have been living on hardtack until I could find a safe place. I want my freedom but I don't want anything to do with the army. I hear there is a place for blacks to learn things on Sea Island. I would do most anything to have a taste of good fish after living on cold hardtack for three days."

The old man said, "Take off your clothes and wade out and hand them to me and them you can go back and get your gear and hand it to me as I come by and them we'll sail on home and at least get a warm meal and you'll have a safe place to sleep."

Macon did as directed and climbed into the boat after he had handed over his clothes and his gear. The old man gave him his clothes and he got dressed as they tacked along the shore. Macon learned they were in the Potomac River but near enough to its meeting with the ocean that the tide and the fish flowed in and out twice a day. He told the fisherman about helping young Dan bring supplies to Richmond and then going with Dan to drive the ambulance until Dan was called back to his company. He described what he and Dan had seen as they hauled the wounded to the doctors. That had been enough; he did not want to be in either of the armies. The fisherman was surprised to learn the Confederates were thinking about taking slaves into their army as the Federals had. Macon said as far as he knew they did not have any black companies but they were using all they could get in units where they would not be in the thick of the fighting.

The fisherman said my name is Frank and, "I'll drop you off at my dock while I go into town to sell the fish. Two of the fish will be enough for our supper. The fish is a flounder and makes good eating." They pulled to his dock and Macon unloaded his gear and Frank handed him two of the fish and Macon's knife and showed him how to clean the fish. Macon had not seen Frank frisk his clothes for the knife but guessed he had found it when he turned back to load his gear aboard the boat. Frank may be old but he's still sharp and agile thought Macon.

Frank said, "My house is on up the trail about a hundred yards. You will find the door open. Inside, you'll find a pan at the house to use while you clean the fish. I'll be back in about an hour."

Macon took the fish and his gear up the trail and found a small cabin with a latch string on the door. He set his gear down against the wall and looked for a pan to put the fish in. The cabin was neat and clean with a dirt floor that had been swept until it looked like pavement. He found the well and pulled up a bucket of water as sweet as any he had ever tasted. He had not realized how thirsty he had gotten with all the excitement and the new experiences that had been coming his way on this day. He suddenly began to feel a strange tingling in his body and he wanted to run and shout "I'm free" but he thought I should keep calm. "I could have been in trouble this afternoon because I got carried away with seeing new things and didn't watch the birds. But what a wonderful feeling it is."

He cleaned the fish and drew another bucket of water for the house and then began to look around the yard. There was a vegetable garden and Macon was busy pulling weeds when Frank returned. Frank noted this fellow seems sharp and he surely is not lazy. "Maybe I can help him." He started a fire in his stove and made supper for them which tasted better than anything Macon had enjoyed since he had left home.

After dinner, they began to explore each other's background and experiences. Frank's owner had left Maryland shortly after the war had started and had left Frank and his wife to look after the home place. The owner took the rest of the slaves to their other place in Georgia. A few months later the Federal forces had taken the home place for their own use as confiscated property of a rebel. They let Frank and his wife use this cabin as their own and told them they were free. His wife had died about a year ago and he had been living alone since then. His contact in town was with a restaurant that wanted fresh fish each day. This made a way for him to get needed things on the outside. The vegetables he grew on his plot gave him something to do when he was not fishing and made for meals he liked. One of the deacons of his church was going to give him some baby chickens and a young pig. He thought he had a good but lonely life. He did not know what had happened to his children because the owner had taken them with him to Georgia.

Macon told Frank about his life in Virginia and his relationship with young Dan who had been the one to tell him about Sea Island and teaching him how to shoot and to write his name. He sure missed his mom but it looked to him like there was going to be much trouble in Virginia and his best chance of learning how to read and write was to get to Sea Island.

Frank said, "I don't blame you for not wanting to be in the army, I hear they only get half pay and the worst assignments. Just because the North is freeing the slaves does not mean the Northern people like the blacks. They don't accept them as equals and have been known to be exceedingly cruel in some locations. Just because they consider I'm free does not mean I can do as they do or that I have the right to do what I want to do. You are welcome to stay here until you get your feet on the ground and see what you can do about getting to Georgia. It's not a very exciting life but you can learn how to sail and fish and our pastor may be able to help you find a way to get to Georgia."

Macon found his new life was pleasant and he and Frank found enjoyment in being together. He was learning more each day about sailing and fishing and the church had begun classes on three nights a week. He was beginning to learn to read and write something. He found it was slow and difficult to learn to read; it was no wonder Dan liked hunting better than attending to his school work. He was determined he would stick with it until he could read and write. The preacher thought Macon was making good progress but it seemed slow and difficult to Macon. Frank took the classes with him for awhile and then stopped. He loved to have Macon read to him and it turned out to be a help for Macon as it made him struggle more to be able to please Frank.

Macon learned how to observe the weather signs, to head for home when a storm was brewing and was honing his skills at fishing and sailing. The young chickens began to grow at a surprising rate and he and Frank could count the days until they would have their own fried chicken. Frank said we also will have some of our own fresh eggs before fall and when the cold weather rolls around we will have a hog to turn into ham and bacon and sausage. The rains came at the right time. Their garden was producing a bountiful crop and it looked like it would carry them into the fall.

Days seemed to follow days in a succession of pleasant experiences for Macon. He was learning many things from Frank and from the church group. The minister's classes in reading and writing were very popular and then as the older ones dropped out, the class became one for youngsters with Macon being the oldest student. He felt embarrassed to be in the class with the kids and almost dropped out. The minister told him how important it was for him to stay and learn and offered to give him private lessons if he could not take the contrast in size and age. Macon thought, "A lot worse things have happen to me. I can take this because I'm learning something that'll be useful."

Frank began to take Macon to the restaurant where he sold his fish and to the grocery store where he bought the few staples they needed. Macon knew enough to follow Frank's lead when they dealt with the whites but could hardly wait until they got home for an explanation. Macon could not comprehend why they had to continue slave-day mannerisms if they were free.

Frank said, "I think you should discuss that with our minister. If you want to succeed and get what you want, you should learn to do as I do. I'm not saying I think it's right; it's just the way things are and I don't think you and I'll change the way other people act."

Macon and the minister had a long session trying to get to an understanding of why they were free but not equal. The minister explained most people who had pressed ardently for freeing the slaves did not think the freedmen should be considered the equal of the whites. The most radical abolitionists did not think the freedmen should be allowed to vote or to serve on a jury. Some suggested the freedmen could be brought to the point where they could be expected to be "responsible citizens." The minister thought this was wrong and they might be able to present a case for fair treatment but you had to accept the world for the way it was and work for a better day.

"I'm sure you know the old saying, 'When you ain't got, you have to make do.' That's where we are today and it may be a long long time before we or our children see any progress to being free and equal. We have to prepare for progress and understanding by educating ourselves and others. Nature's law sometimes seems cruel but the fittest always survive and the persecuted will become the victors. If the world were perfect, it might be fair but for now, it's a long way from being fair."

As the year moved into fall, they began to hear rumors Grant had backed Lee into a defensive position around Richmond and the Federals were beginning to shatter the South's ability to take the offensive. The traffic on the river was greater than any other time Frank could remember. Their part of the world seemed to be on a side track where they could see great things were in progress without being a part of the action. They began to harvest oysters and continued to catch flounders. Macon thought he had never tasted anything better than fried chicken until Frank fixed him his first taste of fried oysters.

Their garden produced a bumper crop of potatoes and Frank showed Macon how to store them by using the corn stalks to protect them from the soil. Frank explained that this type of storage for winter use was called banking. Their chickens had supplied an occasional dinner earlier in the year and now began to provide eggs. They were looking for a good cold snap in December when they would slaughter their pig to add to their winter food. Macon and Frank went over his session with the minister repeatedly trying to find how they could change the way the world was treating the "freedmen." Frank led Macon through the process to show if they resorted to active opposition, they always invited a violent reaction. They knew Negro bodies found their way into the river and no one ever bothered to make an investigation to find out how they got there.

They were overjoyed to hear Lee had surrendered. The minister and the congregation prayed for the troubled land to return to peace and justice. They were dashed to the point of despair in less than a week to learn Lincoln had been assassinated. "Mas" Lincoln had been their symbol of deliverance and now he had been cut down. The whole church mourned the loss but Frank seemed to take it as the last straw the world had dealt him. He could not understand how the Lord could allow such a good man to be cut down by a crazy actor. Within a month, he was a shell of his former self. He grieved about the loss of Lincoln and could not understand why his children would not come back to the home place to take care of their father. No one could convince him there might be valid reasons his children did not promptly return to the home place. He told Macon he wanted him to take the boat south and see if he could find his children after his death. This frightened Macon as he did not believe anyone who had been so resourceful such a short time ago could just decide to give up. He had the minister over hoping he could bring Frank out of his depression. Frank repeated his instructions about what he wanted Macon to do and asked the minister to see that Macon carried out his wish. A week later he died.

Now it was Macon's turn to be depressed. The interlude with Frank had been a pleasant time and he had learned from Frank and the others in the area. He thought he had to honor Frank's wish but about the last thing he wanted to do was to leave the good life he had found. He owed so much to that good man. The minister helped him by telling him the general area where he might look for Frank's children and suggested he stay in touch with the Negro churches as he traveled. They would be a source of information and help. He should try to get the boat to the Savannah area and if after searching there for some time, he might look to the islands on down the coast. The minister thought from what he had heard

Macon might find the Savannah area more to his liking than Sea Island which had been Macon's original goal.

Reluctantly, Macon gathered up Frank's few belongings and packed his gear for the trip. The minister and most of the congregation were on the dock to wish him Godspeed as he sailed out.

CHAPTER XIII

Homefront, 1864

THE trip back home for the Woottons and Daniel Johns was anything but a cheerful trip. The rain continued to come down in a light drizzle and it seemed to depress the three people more than the pain of parting with the young buck. Each in his own heart knew there was danger ahead for their son and grandson and that the war was not going well for the South. The fact the authorities would have the Johns and the Woottons trade cotton for needed supplies said the Northern superiority in men and material was twisting the knot tighter around the throat of the South. No one would discuss the possibility the South was on a losing course but each in his own thoughts believed it was a fair possibility. They might have excellent generals but they had to have men and material to complete their missions. Some day, the 2,000,000 men in the Northern armies would get generals competent enough to make life miserable for the South's 600,000.

Daniel Johns asked them to stop and have supper with him but Martha said she was tired and told Kitty they would be back before the little ones had to be put to bed. As much as Martha loved both of the men, she knew they wanted to be alone with their thoughts and this was a good time to keep everyone in his own niche without risking a stressful evening. The two men had been closer during this war than ever before but there was no reason to believe their relationship had matured. At best, it was an armed truce and they did not need stressful times to break out into warfare again.

Eva had a cup of hot coffee laced with brandy when Daniel Johns got to his study. Daniel thought, "This woman always seems to know when I need a good cup of coffee with black cream. I'm lucky to have such a good servant. I must spend some time trying to piece together what may happen if the Yankees do win this war. As terrible as I think such a happening would be for our culture, we must expect a sudden and complete disruption of all our lives until some order is restored."

Eva broke into his musing to announce the cook had a good hot bowl of potato soup ready if that met his pleasure. He thought, "She's a jewel in more ways than one."

Daniel Johns took his runabout into Green Bay the next day and discovered there were more shortages than the week before and the Confederate currency had been devalued by one third for bills over $5.00 face value. Daniel thought the general inflation and the scarcity of some items is bad enough. Davis seems to have lost control or his senses; maybe both.

Martha brought over a note from young Daniel that told them he and Macon had been met on the outskirts of Richmond and he and Macon had been assigned to Hood's brigade as ambulance drivers. He was getting good hot food and was trying to exercise his leg each day; he hoped to get into shape to rejoin his unit. The next note they received said the Grant offense was taking its toll and young Dan had returned to his unit on May 7.

Daniel Johns got the first information from the station master. The Yankee cavalry had made a raid into the outskirts of Richmond and the Confederate great, General Stuart, had been killed at Yellow Tavern. Tom made a contact with his sources on the nineteenth of May and found Stuart had been killed in the raid and young Dan had been captured at Spottsylvania. The cavalry raid had been costly to both sides but probably more so to the South because they lost Stuart. Young Dan had been captured on May 12 when General Hancock used a very foggy morning in some fashion to capture General Johnson and forced him to surrender his whole command. This coup captured three generals, fifty other officers and 3,000 troops. The Federals were so busy getting their haul away that Lee countered what could have been a disastrous breakthrough. Tom and his colleagues had no way of understanding how General Johnson could have been surprised by Hancock or if he had been taken by a sneak raid why he would surrender his whole command. They later learned it was not a sneak raid but a major push by Hancock's forces which cleverly used the dense fog as a cover to take Johnson's whole command by surprise.

By the end of May, Tom found young Dan and thousands of other prisoners were being held in Maryland near Point Lookout. It made a convenient place to transport and guard prisoners and was nearby if the prisoners were to be exchanged.

June brought no better news. The battle around Richmond was bloody and costly to both sides but the South did not have the resources to replace their losses. Grant seemed to be immune to the carnage he was causing and kept the pressure on Lee. Sheridan's ride around Richmond brought terror to the civilian population but Sherman's march into Georgia did not excite nearly as much editorial comment. Tom thought Sheridan's raid was important but not as dangerous to the South as Sherman's march through Georgia. Tom and Daniel Johns debated what Lee and Davis should do about defending Richmond. It was not good strategy for Lee to be tied down; his forte had been the ability to gain advantage by terrain and surprise. But, it was not practical to abandon Richmond and it was dangerous politically to try at this late date to move the Confederate capitol. Moving the capitol had been an emotional decision and popular with the masses but it had been a strategic mistake then and was a real problem now. Davis either decided the political risks were too great or as Tom and Daniel believed, Davis did not decide the issue, hoping the problem would go away.

Tom's contact reported the discussion in Richmond centered on hoping Lincoln would not be renominated. Davis and his advisors could read the New York papers and take courage; maybe the North would reject Lincoln and his conduct of the bloody war. He could lose the election. Daniel Johns thought this was the craziest idea Davis and his crew stumbled on. Everyone knew Greeley thought that he, Greeley, should have been President. Davis and the other leaders in Richmond took Greeley's howling comments as a ground swell of support for him. Tom and Daniel thought this was like believing in your own dreams or having someone read tea leaves. Lincoln's nomination in early June did not stay the dreaming.

From this background, it made sense to send General Early on a raid towards Washington. He might garner some needed supplies from the countryside and the raid might relieve some pressure on Lee at Richmond. It had worked to destroy the plans of Union generals before and any other option seemed too painful. Tom and Daniel thought the tactic would not work this time and the progress Sherman was making in Georgia as Johnson retreated could have received more attention than it was getting in Richmond. Tom pointed out when you became trapped with the defense of Richmond, you lost sight of the general problem; the political problem with losing your capitol had to take back seat to your ability to keep a fighting force in being. Davis could not take the risk, could not see the problem, or more probably could not admit he might have made an error in locating the capitol in Richmond. Daniel thought the latter point was the cardinal one with Davis; pride was a great thing and good motivation for human progress but it could damage a person's ability when allowed to get out of hand. Tom commented Davis had always been blessed with more pride than ability; Daniel thought it was beginning to appear to be true.

July brought more disturbing developments. Sherman continued his march through Georgia and occupied Marietta. Greeley's push for peace talks turned into a dud when the Southern representatives turned out to be wishful dreamers and mid-July brought the news the prisoners were not being exchanged because of disputes about captured Negro troops and the repugnance of the South to deal with General Burnside who had been assigned this role. The great secret scheme, to outfit two ships and run guns to the prisoners at Point Lookout, had to be abandoned when the news was printed in Northern newspapers. Tom was disgusted that anyone would plan such a foolish project. The idea you could keep anything a secret in Richmond had been proved ridiculous time and time again. At month-end, they learned Sherman was before Atlanta. Davis replaced General Albert Sidney Johnson with General Hood, and Hood began making preparations for the abandonment of Atlanta. The Federals set off a huge explosion under the Confederate lines near Richmond but did not press their advantage and lost the day. There were wild rumors about Davis being insane and one as wild that Lincoln was ready to resign.

August's most disturbing news to the Wootton and the Johns households was the movement of the prisoners at Point Lookout to Elmira, New York. Tom checked and found a new stockade had been built there. The result of the news about the plan of a raid to release the prisoners at Point Lookout caused the prisoners to be shipped to Elmira. The chance for a prisoner exchange was dim and the Federals thought they should house them in a location where they would not be a temptation for a raid. Later in the month, Tom got the news Admiral Farragut had captured Mobile. They read in the northern papers General Grant had ordered General Sheridan to raid the Shenandoah valley and to leave the valley stripped to where a "crow flying over the valley will have to carry his own rations." Tom thought those poor people in the valley will now pay for Early's raid into the Washington area.

The fall of Atlanta began the month of September on a bad note. There was not much else in the outlook to make for bright hopes. Daniel Johns found the Confederate currency was becoming more and more unreliable and he could trade bacon for weaving and turnip seed for sugar. With the Confederate hopes being dashed for a military victory, their currency was being beaten down at the same rate. There were wild hopes Lincoln might not be re-elected; his successor would negotiate an end to the war. Daniel Johns thought this had to be another of those bourbon dreams wandering around Richmond.

Early in October, the Confederates ordered the women and children out of Petersburg as the area was subject to artillery shelling and they had no way of protecting them. Soon after, everyone was overjoyed to hear from General Early that he had defeated Sheridan; then in a few days their emotions were dashed against the real report. Early only thought he had defeated the Yankees and Sheridan's counterattack was so successful the entire valley had been left to the Federals.

The Federal Congress convened after Lincoln's re-election with the Republicans in firm control. The Senate had been stung by Lincoln's pocket veto of their reconstruction bill. Lincoln thought he could make the re-admission of the Confederate states on a pattern to his liking. The radical Republicans were determined they were going to be the ones to set the program for the return of the rebels. At stake was the control of Congress or more to the point, the continued control of Congress by the radical Republicans who now chaired the committees. They could see the possibility the rebels would return and combine with the northern Democrats to wrest control away. Senator Summer developed the precept of "state suicide" to justify his actions. Control in the rebel states had to be turned to the Republicans via the enfranchisement of the slaves. Daniel Johns reminded both Tom and Martha that Senator Summer was the one Preston Brooks beat with Summer's own cane in 1856. The caning nearly killed Summer and crystallized the North determination. It equally became the rally cry of the South. Hundreds of canes were shipped to Brooks with the implied thought that if he had used a Southern cane he would have been successful in completing his job without breaking the cane. Summer's concept that the Negro be allowed to vote in southern states did not square with the practice in his state, Massachusetts, and other northern states where Negroes were not allowed to vote. Such inconsistency did not offset the pressing need to assure the Republicans remain in control of Congress. Summer and others could disregard such matters for now; they were determined they were not going to pass the control of Congress to the rebels. From Summer's point of view, they had struggled long and hard to produce defeat of the South. It was the soldiers who had done the struggling and Congress labored over a hot desk. The urgent matter was staying in control of Congress.

Martha had never seen the two men as worked up over anything as the news Davis and Lee were considering the conscription of Negroes for war service. Tom could not believe anyone in his right mind would even think of such an outrageous idea, much less propose it be considered. Davis proposed that 40,000 slaves be recruited to serve as laborers and engineers and to serve as a nucleus for an armed group as and when needed. They assumed the promise of freedom would be the attraction for the Negroes. Tom thought the rumor of last summer that Davis was insane was more true than he and Daniel thought. As with most hot ideas, Davis and his advisors had not considered how the slave owners were to be compensated nor many other questions. The accepted dogma, the Negro was best served to be a slave, had received much support from their preachers. This belief that the South's peculiar institution was God's way of caring for an inferior race could not be discarded on a whim.

Sherman's abandonment of his base at Atlanta and his supply line after forcing the residents of Atlanta to leave and burning the city seemed the height of barbarian conduct to Martha and Daniel Johns. Tom thought to himself, I better not make any comment because I could never fend off the two of them but this may be a very shrewd move Grant and Sherman have worked out. War is never a pleasant thing and the destruction of Atlanta could be viewed as a war-time necessity. It is hell for the people involved but the loser always gets into trauma of some kind and often, so does the victor.

A few days after Christmas they received the news Sherman had taken Savannah. By the end of the year, they painfully were aware Lee had forwarded his recommendation to Davis for the South to conscript 200,000 Negroes and train them and arm them for combat service. Both Daniel and Tom agreed that only the knowledge the war was lost would have made anyone seriously consider such a proposal. It was time for them to start thinking about what was going to happen in the next few days, weeks, or months they had left before the fire-storm swept over them. This was not going to be a case of how to continue their lifestyle but on what they could do to survive.

Daniel Johns thought, "I began with nothing and I may end life the same way. It's hard for me but in some ways it's harder for Martha and Tom because they have never known what it's like to really have nothing and to have to scratch for survival. Lord knows how many crazy things we'll do to be able to exist, let alone to live as we would like."

January brought a sharp cold snap on the 9th and this brought on the furious activity of turning hogs into their food products. No one had time for anything but hog processing for days. The slaughter, the hot kettles of water for scalding the carcass, the rendering process for lard and the joy everyone had in crackling bread, and the more tedious process of smoking hams and sausage and curing bacon occupied both owner and slave.

Daniel thought, "I have to get this done and get it behind me, so I can plan how to conserve and safeguard this food when the bad days start banging around our heads. The first thing I must do is to build a strong and secure store room. I think it'll have to be mostly underground. That way it will not be subjected to being torched and will have a degree of temperature control. I should locate it where I can cover its entrance from the house; if times get as unruly as they might, I may have to let someone have a taste of buckshot. It seems odd to be planning on steps just to have something to eat. I hope this is the worst problem we'll have but I'm sure there will be ones we think are more serious."

The criticism of Davis and his apparent preference for Bragg, who everyone thought was a loser, reached a peak. There was open talk of deposing Davis. Davis who was deaf to some things, could hear this comment and in January appointed Lee as the Commander-in-Chief. Tom and Daniel thought if Lee should really try to be the Commander-in-Chief, Davis would have to invent some reason to sack him. They thought Lee understood the situation and did not want to become the lighting rod for the failure already on them. But this neither Davis nor Lee could admit.

They were not surprised to hear in early February about Davis dispatching Vice President Stephens, Hunter and Judge Campbell on a peace mission. Since Stephens was the leader of the opposition to Davis, they were not sure Davis had authorized the try or had acquiesced to it because he could not stop it. They were not surprised that Stephens could not find any common ground with Lincoln's position, the states would return subject to the Federal constitution; i.e., the freeing of the slaves. Stephens had made his position clear early in the war when he talked about the difference between the North and the South. He stated the Northern position was for people to be free and equal; the Southern government was formed in the belief the Negroes were not equal. As far as Davis and Stephens and most Southern politicians were concerned, they might be able to talk about arrangements for the slaves being free but never in the world could they accept the thought they might be equal. They had listened for years to their religious leaders as they expounded on the biblical background for the support of slavery. Daniel thought politicians have always responded to a posture which brought in money and maybe our ministers are not far advanced from the same temptation. They should learn to read a different Bible Daniel said to himself because it would have been dangerous to let his peers know what his thoughts were in the matter.

February also brought the news Sherman was ready to take Columbia and the Confederates had evacuated Charleston. The Confederate Congress was planning to pass the measure to enlist slaves in the Confederate army and the result was many able-bodied male slaves left for the Federal lines. They might not want to join the Federal army but this was a better option than to stay in place and to be put in the Confederate army. Most of the congressional members were amazed their slaves would take such action.

Daniel had been required by congressional fiat to pay 10% of his produce to the central government and had been forced to pay his taxes in produce when the central government refused to accept their bonds as payment.

Daniel thought, "I'll be darned if I part with the piddling amount of gold I have been able to hide."

By the end of March, two agents appeared with the authority of the provost marshal to requisition horses and other supplies for the Confederate forces. Daniel had no way of verifying the agents really had the authority or whether they had bogus papers. Daniel acted as though he thought the two were real patriots and as much as he hated to part with his work stock and the food, he professed it was his duty to save the cause and he would comply.

As the two left Daniel Johns' yard with his wagons and stock, he gave them each a bottle of brandy for their personal use. He assured them he knew they would not use any of their "requisitioned" products for their own use, so this was a present for their patriotic efforts in the cause of justice. Before the day was out, the railroad agent drove into Daniel's yard with the information the two had been trying to sell him one of Daniel's mares. Daniel thanked the agent and got his guns and Tom and started after the two. They found them camped west of town and in a drunken stupor after having emptied the brandy bottles. Tom thought the proof pointed to a couple of deserters who were trying to feather their nest on the way to their homes in the mountains of North Carolina.

He thought they should shoot them on the spot but Daniel said, "Let's take their clothes and burn them. As we leave, we can tie them to a tree and let them get free sometime later. I don't think they'll bother us again. I don't know what they'll do as barefoot and naked travelers but they'll have something else to think about other than conning people out of their food and animals."

They got home with the wagons and the animals about daylight and heard the rumor as they passed through town that Lee was abandoning Richmond and Davis and the cabinet were fleeing. Later in the week they were aware that Lee and his worn out troops were passing to the north of them and Lee had been stopped and had surrendered nearby at Appomattox. Daniel Johns got Tom and Martha together to tell them what he was going to do since the Confederacy was doomed. Davis and a few of his people were trying to flee to Georgia or Florida with hope the conflict was not yet ended. Tom said this confirmed Davis was a dreamer to the end because he told people less than a week ago if he took one army and Lee the other, the two of them still would bring off a victory for the South. Tom thought Davis had been true to the pattern that could have been predicted but to give the devil his due, maybe no one could have pulled the various states into a unit that could have won. The vicious attacks by most of the state governors and the sniping headed by Vice President Stephans did not help the Confederate cause.

Daniel sent for Eva and told her to get Sam. He told them he wanted all the slaves to appear at the house the next morning. He told them what he proposed to tell the slaves; they were free or soon would be by army fiat or other means. No one knew just what was going to happen but one fact was clear; they were no longer his property. He proposed to care for them and to feed them as he had formerly until other arrangements had been developed. He thought arrangements would be made soon for payment for their work or for sharing in the crops produced. He was aware of the rumor the slaves were to be supplied with forty acres and a mule. He thought such a prospect was never going to come into being. If they chose to go to other locations, they were free to do so but they would not be allowed to return to his property. They should understand if they did not work, they would not eat or be clothed or be permitted to remain in his houses. They should be overjoyed with the news but they also should think about some hazards that might await them; one particularly, since they were no longer the property of anyone there was no inhibition in damaging or destroying them. He did not want to change any of the long-term relationships which had existed but things were going to change. And maybe not for the best interests of either the Negroes or the whites. Whatever he or they did from this time on was going to be plowing a new field and maybe neither they nor he would be able to do as they might like to do.

The meeting the next morning was an emotional affair; many Negroes wanted to know just what did it mean they were free. Daniel replied, "It may mean many things. One for sure, before you were free, each of you were my property. Some of you would have brought as much as $800 if I had wanted to sell you. That part of my property is now gone; I cannot sell you nor can you sell yourself. We'll have a different relationship since the war has been won by the North. I took care of you as slaves because you were my property. Since you are not my property now, I don't have to take care of you or to feed or nurse you or to provide you with a place to sleep. You are free to leave this place and live where and how you please. If you do leave, I'll not allow you to return. I'll feed, care and house you as I have while you work as you have formerly and we'll work out a system for payment or sharing what we produce that's as good as or better than what others in this area will be doing. No one knows just what rules we'll have until we get a new government. We shall have some turbulent, maybe bad times, before we find out just what this defeat of the Confederate army means. I hope all will make it through these trying times but I cannot promise you we will. What little Confederate money I have is now not worth anything and I don't know when I can get any Federal money. We'll have to live as best we can on what we have and hope things will work out. You should understand when you belonged to me, you had a protection you don't have now. In those days, anyone damaging you would have to answer to me for damaging or destroying my property. Now you do not have that protection. There'll be many people enraged by the changes we will be going through and I hope neither you nor I'll suffer. I cannot do more than to urge you to be cautious. Discuss things among yourselves and I'll be glad to try to answer any questions you have. You know Sam or Eva has my ear. We are compelled to go down a road neither of us has traveled before. I hope it's not bumpy but it well may be."

By the end of April, they received the news of Lincoln's death. Daniel had Sam get the people together and they could all hear about the tragedy. He told them what he knew about the assassination; the Federal forces were trying to capture Booth, the actor who shot Lincoln. He also told them General Johnson had surrendered to General Sherman in North Carolina and the war was over unless some scattered units had not been brought in. Sam asked if they could use one of the vacant buildings for a church and would it be possible to hold classes for reading and writing. Daniel said they could use the old north shed and maybe they should take the rest of the day off to clean it out and get it ready for classes and services.

CHAPTER XIV

The Long Walk

WHEN Dan heard the second whistle, he was sure Macon was in the area. He mused how in the world did Macon get down here in Savannah. Dan turned to the direction of the whistle and there was Macon leaning against the building wall.

Dan and Macon's first questions were the same, "How'd you get down here?"

Dan related the story of his capture and then his imprisonment at Elmira, New York and then the boat ride down the coast.

Macon told about making his way through the lines and then to the coast where he had met Frank and learned how to fish. He said, "It looks like you could stand a good meal, come to my place and I'll fix you a flounder for supper."

Dan said, "Sounds great but I find I'm having trouble walking. I have heard about getting sea legs and I guess that is what happened to me on the boat ride down here. I didn't get seasick as many people did so maybe I'm paying for it by having trouble with walking on land now."

Macon said, "You should stay around here for a few days because from what I hear you'll need steady legs to get you home. There is not much way to get around down here except to walk, unless you have a horse to ride and they come at a dear price. I'll help you get some things you'll need to get home."

Dan replied, "I can remember when you caught those quail we had for breakfast on the ride down to Warrenton. That seems like it was such a long long time ago but I can remember how good they tasted. If the flounder is half as good, you may have to throw me out to get me to leave."

Macon showed Dan the quarters he had developed and the boat he had used to get down the coast. He could make a living with the fishing skills he had learned from Frank. Dan said the food had been pretty bad and skimpy in the army but it really was bad when he got to the stockade.

Macon said, "You'll like this fish and the corn bread with it. We are beginning to get good coffee here now but coffee is one thing you may have had in prison."

Dan thought the fish supper was so good he could have made himself sick from eating too much.

Macon pointed out his bunk in the cabin and said, "You sleep there tonight and I'll sleep in the boat."

Dan said, "Let me sleep in the boat because it's like what I have been doing."

Dan woke the next morning to the smell of the hot coffee Macon had fixed. Dan wanted to know what Macon intended to do. Was he going to live here or was he going back home? Macon explained he had been charged with finding Frank's family who had been sent south at the start of the war. He had found Frank's son and his family and had given them the few things Frank wanted them to have. In traveling down the coast, it seemed to him this was a better part of the country. The fishing he liked much better than farming. Also, he found Frank had a pretty granddaughter and they expected to get married soon. He would like to see his mother but he felt his life would be better here than in Virginia. "It doesn't get near as cold down here as it does in Virginia. Before too long, they'll repair the railroads and maybe mama Kitty can come down to see me and her new daughter-in-law."

Macon said, "You'll need a knife to go in your boot scabbard because I'm sure they did not let you keep yours in the stockade and you'll need matches and other things to make it home. There are some mean people out there now. They tell me you need to be cautious where you spend the night. The whole country is in very bad shape and you probably will find no one has much to spare. You are lucky you have those good boots Sam made for you. There are people about who would harm you to get boots. After a day or two of good food and rest, you should be in shape to make the trip. It'll not be like the trip we had with Maude and Dolly to ride but you may find things better than I think they may be. When Sherman went north from here, we hear there was not much left for anybody."

Dan and Macon spent the next two days getting things Dan would need on the trip back to Virginia and as far as Dan was concerned he was getting his legs back in shape for the walk. Macon's food was as good therapy for his body as his kind treatment was for his mind. Macon found a blacksmith who made Dan a knife he could carry in his boot scabbard and Macon had an old sail they could convert into a tarpaulin. Somehow a blanket turned up and a supply of hardtack. Dan never questioned Macon about how he could get these things but was thankful he was getting what he needed to make his walk possible.

Dan mused, "I think it was June 21 when they put me on the train to New York, June 23 when they put us on the boat and we got here in Savannah on Friday, June 30. I'll get started early Monday morning, July 3 and if I keep at it I should be in Green Bay by the first of August. I think I'll make for Florence, Fayetteville, by Raleigh and into Warrenton and on home. There is no use thinking about going by the Atlanta road because you know Sherman did not leave anything there and it may be slim pickings anywhere on the trip."

It was an emotional farewell the next morning. Macon gave Dan a letter to give to his mother saying she probably would not be able to read it but Dan or someone could read it to her. It was his way of telling his mother about the progress he had made since she had seen him and something he was sure she would like to keep.

Dan said, "This trip will never end if I don't put one foot in front of the other one and get started. It's been great seeing you and my thanks for the things you have done for me. Kitty will get your letter. I'll enjoy telling her about the great progress you have made and the pretty little girl who will soon be your bride. I hope we meet some day and I can help you as you have helped me. I have no idea how things will be at home nor what I'll do after I get there but I have to see the family."

Dan hoisted his tarpaulin roll over his shoulder and started down the road to Florence. He hoped he could make it in the first week or less. As he was ready to turn the first corner, he paused and took one last look at Macon standing by his shack and gave his two-tone whistle and Macon replied with the same signal. Dan thought, "He's a good man, even if he is a Negro and he's been my friend since the earliest days I can remember. I don't know what life will hold for either of us but I should like to know how he does."

Dan found the walk boring, dusty, and hot. It wasn't the same as the marching he had done on the forays in Maryland and into Pennsylvania. What a long time ago it seemed. Then, the excitement of the army moving into enemy territory and the insistent demand of Lee and Jackson made the walking go faster. Now, he had a bad leg from the Gettysburg wound and the group pressure to perform was missing.

The countryside was a wreck where Sherman's boys had foraged. He found burned out barns and houses they had left behind and the people were left with nothing. Some were trying to eke out a living by starting over; some had abandoned their places and moved to other locations. More often than not the newly freed Negroes had gathered around the villages and towns waiting for what they thought was the promise of forty acres and a mule. Some of them found they could get an occasional food handout from the Federals but for the most part, they just wandered about and made do with whatever food they could scrounge. Rarely did he find an owner who had been able to keep some of his former slaves on his farm working in some semblance of their former activity. Both Negroes and land owners seemed to be trying to make an adjustment to conditions neither had faced before.

Somewhere along the way Dan heard Jefferson Davis had been captured and taken to Fortress Monroe. He remembered seeing the fort across the way when he served at Norfolk at the start of his service. Sometime later he heard the Federals had shackled Davis. It was about this time Dan found that damn-Yankees was one word; he was surprised it rolled off the tongue easily and what a soul-satisfying feeling he got in mouthing it as one word.

Day followed day with the boring drudgery of walking home. He was joined on part of the trip by a fellow Confederate who was trying to get to his home near Garner, North Carolina. The company made the days pass a little bit better than the lone hike and they were fortunate enough to find an old mare in the road. Between the two of them, they caught the mare and Dan made a hackamore from vines. It was unlike riding Maude or Dolly but for the better part of a day they got to ride instead of walk. When they got to Garner, they were in need of a good bath and some hot food. Dan stayed for two days and they pressed him to stay longer but he felt they didn't have enough to really share with others and he needed to get to Warrenton and from there to Green Bay.

The two nights in a bed instead of a barn or just on the ground near a camp fire did a lot for his spirits and he hiked with a new outlook. It wasn't long to Warrenton where he thought he should stop and see how many of the company had made it back. There were many who would never be coming back. He got into the Warrenton area near the end of July and found the old campground where they had first camped and drilled. He camped there instead of going into town. It felt like he was visiting with those who had once been his companions and he wanted the time to review the things he had experienced in the four years since they had all been so young and so sure their cause was right. Maybe their cause had been right and just but he mused, they had not been able to prevail and it did not matter whether their cause had been right or wrong. We have spent four years in a cause that no longer exists and the best thing I can do is to put the time behind me and live for the future.

Dan stopped in the town and found to his surprise Captain Wade was back at the drug store. He had ended the war as a Colonel and told Dan there were only a handful who had made it through the war. He thought the number would be less than ten out of the more than one hundred who had been together in 1861. The defeat was tragedy enough but the real tragedy was the seed corn the South had wasted on the war. The North lost about six percent of their young men but the South lost twenty-three percent of their young men.

Dan thought, "That's part of what I went through last night at the fair grounds. I may have wasted four years and part of a leg but at least I'm here and the only thing to do is to put it behind us and try to continue."

Captain Wade wanted Dan to go home with him for dinner and Dan thanked him but said he thought he should get as far as he could toward home. Wade said he understood and he hoped things would be better for them the next time they met.

Dan followed the route he and Macon had traveled four years before from Warrenton to Green Bay. It took him a lot longer and he could not help thinking, "If it hadn't been for so many of those damn-Yankees, I might have been coming home in style." He had to remind himself he had agreed to forget the past and try to think about the future. He found the spring where he and Macon had camped overnight and discovered the quail runs still existed along the creek. He made a snare and had a good breakfast; it wasn't quite the same without Macon but he got an early start. He hoped he could make it into Green Bay in two more days. That brought back the memory of the time he had been returning from Gettysburg and found Macon at the train station. It suddenly dawned on him he had seen or heard very few trains on his walk from Georgia. He assumed the Federals would get them running in due time but there would not have been much left of the South's rail system. Both sides had burned or blown up plenty of railroad property. He could remember the trouble the South was having with both manpower to run the system and the sad state of repair that existed more than a year ago. He was sure it had not gotten any better in the time he had been a guest of the damn-Yankees. You know, he mused, that damn-Yankee thing is the best thing I have thought of in some time; damn-Yankee, damn-Yankee, damn-Yankee.

"My old bad leg does not hurt as bad after the outburst and I'm sure I can make it to Green Bay sometime tomorrow. I'm not sure what day this is but it does not make much difference. At least, I'm not in a damn-Yankee stockade. I wonder if Grandpa Johns' friend is still the railroad agent. I'll stop by there and see if there is any news I should know before I continue out."

Dan spent the night on a farmer's porch near Victoria, Virginia. The man told Dan his five slaves had left and gone to town when they heard they were free. He could barely manage on what he had been able to keep the Negroes from taking with them as they left. He and his wife were doing what they could to keep the place going but they had no money and did not see how they were going to get a crop in. They did have a garden and they were learning to make do with what they had. At that, they thought they were better off than some larger places. One of their neighbors up the road had two hundred slaves and they all left him within two weeks after the surrender. Neither he nor his wife had ever done anything and they did not know what to do. They came down here begging food because they were hungry and did not know how to cook. "We suggested they should learn as we did not see how they would survive, unless they learned how to take care of themselves. They seemed stunned because everyone had left them and could not understand how the slaves could do that to them. At least we always have worked and while we do not like losing our slaves, we at least know how to take care of ourselves. It is not pleasant having to start over but we are better able to adjust than our neighbors. We think they will give up and go live with some relatives in Georgia."

Dan struggled into Green Bay after a long day's hike in the hot sun. He found the railroad station deserted and eased his bed-roll down in the shade, while he looked for some water to drink and a chance to wash. He found a horse trough and soaked his hot sweaty head in it. As he got back to the station, he found the station master and had to tell him who he was.

The master gave him a cool drink and said, "You rest here 'til I go home and get my buggy and I'll take you out to your grandfather's house. I think your father and mother are on a trip trying to find what has happened to you. I don't know if they are back but your grandpa was in here just a day or two ago to take his oath of allegiance. All of us have to follow the damnest asinine regulations the army hands out."

Dan wanted to know how he could close up the station. "No one knows when a train is coming and there hasn't been one all day. Besides, I've not had any pay for the last three months and not much for the year before that. If it had not been for people like your grandfather, I would have starved long ago. Your grandfather and your parents have all been very worried about you. Some people in other stockades have been back for several months. The people with Lee at Appomattox were here in early April and the others have been coming in since June. They thought you would be here at least by the first of July instead of the first part of August. No one but the Yankees—"

"Damn-Yankees," interrupted Dan.

"That is right. No one but the damn-Yankees would think of the stupid idea of shipping you to Savannah and letting you walk home. You sure have changed since I remember seeing you before the war; sorry that I didn't recognize you but I'm sure Daniel Johns'll be glad to get his namesake home."

Dan wanted to know how things had been here since the war.

The agent said, "From what I hear we're doing better than other areas. I think that your grandfather has lost some of his slaves but for the most part, his people have stayed with him at least until things settle down. Most of the Negroes do not understand what all this means and for sure the damn-Yankees do not know what to do. They have started to send the Negroes back to where they came from and telling them to make a contract with their former owners. That was why Daniel Johns was in town to take the oath of allegiance. No contract will be honored, unless the land owner has been cleared or is a damn-Yankee who came down here and bought property."

Dan was surprised to hear damn-Yankees were buying property in the South.

The agent said, "The damn-Yankees have the money and we don't so they come down here to pick up property at bargain rates. And I do mean bargain rates. The damn-Yankees have always been shrewd traders. The war ruined many of our people and the damn-Yankees are here to pick the bones."

It was near dusk as they neared the Johns' house and no one saw them coming into the yard. As young Dan knocked on the door, he could hear the scurry of someone's feet as they came to the door. Eva opened the door and screamed for his grandfather.

"Your parents are in the north trying to find you. How did you get here?"

"Walked most of the way from Georgia, Eva. It sure is good to finally get home."

Daniel Johns gave his grandson a bear hug that lifted him off his feet. Young Dan was surprised at the strength his grandfather had.

They tried to get the station master to stay for supper but he said he thought he should get back to his family. Young Dan and his grandfather should have the time to update each other on their experiences.

CHAPTER XV

Bridge Work

DANIEL Johns could not take his eyes off his grandson and they tried to bring each other up-to-date on what had happened in the fourteen months since they had been together. Young Dan told about the capture at Spottsylvania without any of them getting to fire a shot. He did not know how it happened but had heard the Yankees had captured or killed the sentries and had gotten to the General's quarters before anyone knew they were in peril. Some sentries may have been asleep. Everyone was tired so it could have happened.

Daniel Johns said he had been luckier than others because most of the blacks had decided to stay with him, at least for the time being. "Your mother and father have moved in with me. Kitty is our cook because the one I had decided to take what she thought was a better contract. She found out it wasn't true and wanted to come back but I established a rule at the start if they left I wouldn't let them come back. Eva and Sam help with the school and church we started for the Negroes in the north barn and that means a lot to them. Some of my neighbors are very critical of what I have done. They think a way will be found to put the Negroes back in their place, as they term it. I guess we always will have dreamers who think there's a way to go back to the good old days."

Dan and his grandfather had to laugh about how he seemed to always arrive home in need of a bath and clean clothes. The borrowed clothes might gather a bit here and there but they were clean and comfortable. The security of loving people and good clean food that awaited young Dan was enough to make the nightmare he had been on for the last four years begin to lose its sharp brutal edges. He never would forget the rough experiences he and his friends received nor would he have anything but hatred for the damn-Yankees.

Dan and his grandfather started to eat the chicken Kitty had prepared and as Dan started to tell how he got to Georgia and then about his walk home, he remembered Macon's letter was in his gear somewhere. He told Eva to bring Kitty in so he could tell her about Macon when he returned with the letter. He found the letter, a little worn and soiled as were all his belongings, and returned to the table.

Kitty could not contain her joy. Young Dan was home at last and had found her son living in Georgia. He told Kitty about Macon's experiences and how he got to Savannah. He wants you to know his new life as a fisherman and his plans to marry a girl he has found. "She is a granddaughter of the man who helped him when he crossed the combat lines and made his way to the coast."

Dan found the return to life at his grandfather's household as comforting as it was when he had returned from his prison experience after the Gettysburg battle. In some ways, this experience was more comforting because he knew he did not have to go back into service. The unsettled conditions connected with the post-war times reached its disruptive finger even into the Johns household. He wondered, if we have to struggle with this type of thing in our remote and sheltered area, what a time the people have that were in the war's path, such as northern Virginia and in Richmond. On balance, it was wonderful to be back home and to have the care he was getting, but the future looked even darker than when all he could see was returning to combat. At least there, you knew what you faced; here there was no firm ground on any plane. He and his grandfather had to face down three people who heard the school had been established and came by with the intent to shut it down. In their viewpoint, such action was unwarranted and dangerous. They threatened to burn the barn if the church and the school were not closed.

Dan had noticed his grandfather strapped on his pistol as he left the house each morning. He always had a shotgun and the rifle Dan had given him within easy reach. The events amazed him. The war was not over, it had just changed into something worse. He discussed the events with his grandfather after he was awakened in the middle of the night by a shot gun blast. His grandfather explained the men had apparently returned to fire the school and church building but had not expected to be greeted in so warm a fashion. The last he knew they were beating their horses trying to get out of range. He thought they would grumble and try to win their point in other ways but they would not return in the middle of the night again.

His grandfather explained most people did not understand or did not want to understand what has happened. "The politicians are telling them the freeing of the slaves was an illegal war-time act and will be reversed by the Supreme Court. If the decision doesn't go the right way, the state legislature'll pass laws to effectively put the blacks under control. Most people misjudge the intent of Congress. They believe President Johnson'll bring the states back into the political process almost, as if the war had not happened. No one should believe the people who have been in control of Congress during the war are now going to say that we have had a nice little war and we'll pass control of Congress to the states we have defeated. A way will be found to keep the war-time northern politicians in control of Congress. We have a situation that's unprecedented; it's no wonder people have trouble understanding what has happened. Everyone tries to resist changes they did not cause. And this is so enormous, so out of pattern, some people will not understand it or be able to adjust to it."

The Woottons returned in mid-August. Tom and Martha had traced young Dan from the prison camp to Savannah and stopped on their return from Philadelphia before going to Georgia. Theirs was tumultuous joy at finding him safe at the farm with Grandfather Johns. Young Dan felt the tragedy of the war had made the family into a more closely knit unit. There were still stresses and strains but the emphasis everyone seemed to have was how can we survive.

Young Dan mused, "It's like the army and the prison days, you learn to survive until there may be a better day. Macon used to tell me, 'When you ain't got, you make do.' It looks like we will have many 'make do' days."

By mid-August, Mississippi and other states had decided their most promising recourse was to recant the ordinance of secession and send their members back to Congress. The courts might or might not declare the freeing of the slaves was an illegal war time act but meanwhile they could get their people back to Congress and start passing state laws for control of the Negroes. Daniel Johns and the Woottons discussed these foolish actions. They agreed the North could not allow the black codes to go unchallenged nor would the Northern politicians agree to turn over control of Congress to the southern states. If the British thought the world turned upside down at Yorktown, the Southern states are in for a greater shock at the reaction of the Yankees. They, the states, never will believe they caused the actions sure to follow. Daniel Johns did not know what actions the Federals would take but some way would be found to negate these actions by the Confederates. Congress would not let the South make a mockery of Yankee war efforts.

There were strange crosscurrents in the times. Federal forces were trying to turn control back to the civil authorities but the federal politicians increasingly were aware they would have to take a stand against their president and the military to preserve the gains they had made in the war. One outgrowth was the freed-men's bureau. They were amazed to learn the rations distributed went to the whites in the ratio of five to one and the most common decision from the bureau was for the Negroes to return to their former masters and work out a contract arrangement for their services. Sometimes where the owner had told the Negroes to leave, the owners were forced to take the Negroes back.

Near the end of November, young Dan found several Confederate notes blowing across the road as he was returning from town. He had gone to town for his grandfather to get supplies and had found a contractor was hiring people to rebuild the railroad bridges. The Confederate money blowing across the road seemed like an omen to him. The grace period that had followed the end of the war in the family relationships was beginning to show signs of strain and there did not seem to be much Dan wanted on the farm. The contractor promised $50 a month and board. Dan knew the work was strenuous from his experiences during the war but it was real money and it got him out of the rut he was slipping into.

His decision was greeted with anguish by his mother and by a knowing nod from his grandfather and father who could understand his motivation, though they did want to see him leave again. He thought he would be helping to get the trains back to running again. The pay would come in handy and improved transportation might help the country. He expected to ride the trains back to see them and if he were ever needed at home, he could get back with little delay.

Dan worked on the bridges between Green Bay and Amelia for the first two months. It was an easy trip to get back home and to catch up on the news and the comments his grandfather and father had on the current state of affairs. Young Dan returned home for Christmas and found the discussions were about the Negroes hoping they would be given land. Most of the Negroes did not want to sign contracts for the next year because they felt they would be given a plot of land. Sam and Eva had asked Daniel Johns if there was any truth to the story. No one could trace the source but it was the type of a story that made every ex-slave hope that it might be true. Daniel Johns explained to them the story may have started when the Yankees had to do something with the blacks they found on their hands when they took the Sea Island territory early in the war. Because they had to find a solution to feeding and caring for the blacks who flocked to their lines, they put them on parcels of property. They hoped to solve the problem of what to do with the blacks and to get cotton grown for the northern mills. It was a war-time expedient and was more successful than they had thought it could be. There was only one thing missing; they did not own the land they parceled out. Now that the war was over, they were faced with the painful task of telling the blacks they did not have a right to the property they believed was theirs. Sometimes, the owners were returning and re-establishing their pre-war operations and some properties were bought by Yankees who thought they recognized a bargain. There was a painful and turbulent process happening there and Daniel did not think the federal government had the means or the stomach to put together a program to distribute land and equipment to the blacks there or anywhere else. He told Sam there were more whites than blacks who would like to see a plan developed to give away land and equipment. Sam could check that by asking in the town about the distribution of rations; more rations were being given to more whites than to blacks.

Before young Dan returned to his bridge-rebuilding job, he heard about the Negroes being killed and dumped into the rivers. His father and grandfather said they had heard of the cases and thought it was the result of the transition. In the pre-war days, the slaves were property and an owner might mistreat or destroy his own property but he would not allow anyone else to take his property. Now the safeguard was not present and we have many people who are bitter about the war and a host of other thing they cannot change or accept. Their frustration can boil over at the sight of a Negro who may have nothing to do with their plight but is a ready symbol and can be attacked without danger. They told him about an organization started in Tennessee by a Confederate general that was sweeping across the south. The "knights," as they called themselves, thought they could control the blacks and keep a semblance of the previous power structure together. Daniel Johns and his father did not care for the structure or the activity but thought it would be a force in southern life. It was a form of guerrilla warfare the Yankees would not be able to stop, though they might be able to make some dents in its activities from time to time. The immediate tragedy were the blacks who would be destroyed or cruelly treated to satiate the frustrations others had in trying to cope with a new order.

Daniel Johns discussed with young Dan his thoughts about the current state of affairs or beliefs the southern people were using to cope with the transition. In the first place, nothing in the war's results in any way changed their belief that slavery had been right. There were too many preachers who had expounded the "fact" that slavery was God's order to protect and save the black man. They were beginning to preserve the myth of the happy plantation life because it fed the concept of white supremacy. He thought few people and maybe none could really accept this might have been wrong. The North had won the war but had not changed what people believed. Many people in the North actively supported the war but did not then or now believe the blacks should be granted equal rights.

The Washington paper brought the news that Senator Summers, at age fifty-five, had married a twenty-five year old widow. The guess in the capitol was he would not find her companionship as comfortable as his mother who had been his alter ego until her recent death.

The paper carried a summary of the war, showing the North lost about 6 percent of its young men and the South about 23 percent. They all thought this was the real tragedy of the war, the loss of the nation's seed corn for the next generation, with the South suffering at a rate about four times the rate of the Yankees.

As the months passed, young Dan found his work drifted away from his home area. The railroad rebuilding took its first priority on those lines that carried the most traffic for the Federals. They needed the roads cleared to provide transportation for the army to their key control points, so the work for Dan's firm carried him south and west. It took too long to make the trip back home every week as much as he enjoyed the food and company. He tried to follow the national developments, so he could understand the discourse with his relatives when he did get back. The only time he had to really study the political trends was on Sunday. He found going to hear the fat, chicken-eating ministers rant was as boring now as it had been before the war. He would find papers and use his one leisure day to skim the stories and then devour in detail any article which appeared to give him a drift of what was happening on the national scene.

Dan was amazed at stories in the local papers; reading some accounts, he thought they did not know who won the war. The same type of impression could be found in discussions with the local citizens. For his main source of information, he found he could get the local agent to save whatever papers he got from Washington or New York. The Richmond papers sometimes carried stories that were reprints from Washington papers. By these means, young Dan found the Federal Congress had passed the reconstruction acts in March of 1866 and there had been blood riots in both Memphis and in New Orleans.

By mid-year 1866, Dan found most of the cities he passed through were beginning to recover and business was returning to an almost normal pattern. He found many more damn-Yankees moving south to pick up land at bargain rates. Many people in the country areas were having a bad time coping with the changing patterns. It was a bad summer for both the blacks and the whites. Many whites could not cope or could not get credit to start operations. This made for bargain purchases by the damn-Yankees who thought they could make effective contracts with the blacks. For the most part, the blacks did not see the Yankee owner was any better than a Southern owner. What they wanted was to be the owner but they found few people would risk the ire of the Southern whites by selling to a black.

Young Dan returned home for Christmas in December 1866 to find the main topic of political discussion at the Johns household was the growing differences between Congress and President Johnson. Stevens and Summers, in the house and senate, were doing everything they could to block the president's attempts to return the southern states to their pre-war status. Johnson was as stubborn in his views as Stevens and Summers and inept in his approach to dealing with Congress. His cabinet felt they owed him no allegiance and thought Congress was right in their approach to dealing with the rebel states.

Several rebel states were shaping their post-war governments, as though the war had been an unhappy episode and now it was time to return to the pre-war congressional status. The most blatant case was the state of Georgia as far as Daniel Johns' thoughts ran. They affronted Congress by sending Alexander Hamilton Stephens to Washington as their Senator. Stephens, the Confederate vice-president, had been Jefferson Davis' most ardent critic during the war. This hardly made him acceptable as a post-war senator as far as the congressional leaders were concerned. Daniel Johns thought the selection and the timing could not have been worse for the South. Congress refused to seat Stephens and other similar cases. The southern papers thundered that such acts were illegal and justice demanded the seating of their representatives. Daniel Johns thought it is not what is legal as much as what it takes to keep the control of Congress in the hands of Stevens, Summers and their friends. All during the war, there had been acts that were of doubtful legality but they worked to preserve what was needed, as those in power saw the need.

Summers and Stevens began a series of open attacks on President Johnson. Johnson, in his usual fashion of heightening any criticism, displaced Secretary Stanton with Grant. There was an immediate demand for Johnson's impeachment. The issue and the shape of our government was settled in May when Johnson's impeachment was sustained by one vote. The resulting hatred of Johnson by both the Republicans and the Democrats made for the selection of Grant for president.

Young Dan was saddened to return home in April for the funeral of his Grandfather Wootton. William Taylor Wootton born in 1787 and at eighty, had been feeble but in good health when Dan saw him at Christmas. He had married Elizabeth Parkinson on December 24, 1807. She had died in 1834 and he had been a widower for thirty-three years. Dan had not been as close to his Grandfather Wootton as his Grandfather Johns because his Wootton grandfather was not nearby and seemed much older than Daniel Johns.

Young Dan continued moving with the bridge crew to the south and west. The work was demanding physically but Dan thought it was not as rugged as the marches demanded by Lee and Jackson on those forays into Maryland and Pennsylvania. He was preparing for a return to the warm family group when he received a wire that his mother had died. It was a devastating blow to Dan, to his father and to his grandfather. She had been the fabric that held their lives together. Dan thought his father might make some type of life with some of his brothers. Thomas Ballard Wootton would not remain in the Johns household for many days.

"As hard as it is to lose your mother in your early twenties," he thought, "how lucky I am to have work that takes me out of the daily contact with the stress here at home. I would always be a symbol that his daughter or his wife is gone; they would make me think how much I miss her."

General Grant's nomination in May and election in the fall were to Dan like a storm blowing overhead, while you were sheltered in the lee of a hill. He returned home for Christmas to find the turmoil surrounding Jefferson Davis' trial in Richmond. That was all the conversation in the coaches as he made the train trip home. He found Daniel Johns and Eva making as warm a reception for him as ever. It did not seem to be the same as before. As much as they seemed to love him and want him near, it also seemed he was interrupting their daily routine. His father was not there and was not mentioned. He found from Sam where they thought he was.

Young Dan thought, "I'll make a detour on my way back to the train and see him. There's no need to make for more strain by any other action." As young Dan started to return, the papers ran the headline that President Johnson's Christmas Day's amnesty had freed Jefferson Davis and others. Summers and Stevens made their protests but the amnesty held. They thought there was not time to turn the act around before Grant's inauguration and once they had Grant in office, they would get what they wanted.

Young Dan read about Grant's inauguration as he was moving with the bridge gang to a big job in upper Mississippi. He remembered his Grandfather Johns thought Grant's term would not be to the South's advantage. So far as what he saw, it looked like there would always be plenty of bridges and trestles that needed replacement or repair. He read about the completion of the transcontinental railroad in May of 1869 and thought the job must have taken more bridges and trestles than he could imagine.

By the fall of 1869, he was reading about the corruption in the federal government and in the major northern cities. Boss Tweed was becoming famous beyond the confines of New York City. He read about the attacks Summers was making on Grant.

Young Dan thought, "Maybe Preston Brooks either knew more than we thought about Summers or he did more damage to Summer's mental powers than we thought. It doesn't seem possible he can attack Grant and not do damage to himself."

Young Dan was contemplating returning to Virginia for Christmas. He thought in one way he had to touch base with home. His grandfather was seventy-five and in good health. He looked as though he would live for years. The problem Dan had was the feeling left over from his last trip that he was a visitor instead of a family member. He had made up his mind he would return for a short visit when he got a telegram from his father. It stated Daniel Johns had suffered a stroke and was not expected to survive. Young Dan broke from his camp and returned by train but his grandfather died before he got to Green Bay.

Dan thought, "I'm no longer young Dan anymore. It's a shame I couldn't have been the one to take his place here at the farm."

They returned back home after the funeral. Each wondering in his own way what was going to happen to the farm and the people who had their lives interwoven with Daniel Johns. Dan met for the first time his grandfather's lawyer, a distant cousin named William Wootton. He read Daniel Johns' will to them. The will expressed over and over that Thomas Ballard Wootton was not to have any support or comfort from Daniel Johns' estate. It hadn't been amended after Martha Johns Wootton's death, although it left his estate for her benefit. The property was to be operated for her benefit by the lawyer and the law firm was to receive a seven percent commission on any transaction. Dan got the impression that in a matter of a year or two, the property would be divided between the four children.

CHAPTER XVI

Mississippi

DAN stayed at his grandfather Johns' house for a few days after the funeral. He packed a few things to help remind him about the good times he had with his grandfather. Most of them he did not need or intend to use but there was no point in leaving them to be taken by strangers. The lawyer thought he would have an overseer there within a week and asked Dan to stay until the man arrived.

Dan thought, "Eva and Sam know more about running these places than I do but I want a few days to say goodbye to my youth here."

It was a melancholy time for Dan. He rode the area to take one last look at the town, the hunting areas and all the things that he remembered as pleasant experiences. It all seemed a long time ago; it was eight years but what a change; it seemed like it had been a long long time ago. There was no way to go back and everything here reminded him of what used to be and of the great losses of his mother and grandfather. He rode into Green Bay and bought his ticket for the next day. He could not stay here and live in the past or more to the point, grieve about what had been lost in the eight years. He had to do the same thing he had done with his war experiences, put them behind him and look to what he could do today and tomorrow.

The train ride back to Mississippi was a sad trip. He remembered the old refrain: "Clickity-click, clickity click/ you'll never get rich/ you son of a bitch/ Clickity-click." This time the rails seemed to say; "Clickity-click, clickity-click/ Your youth is gone/ Is gone, is gone/ Clickity-click." He sat, as though he was in a trance, noticing but not responding to what was happening around him. There had been the emotional parting with Kitty and Eva at the house and an equally upsetting parting with Sam at the station. They were good people.

"If I could have been the man Daniel Johns wanted me to be, I'd still be there with them. I wasn't what he wanted and there is nothing to be gained by wishing or trying to force myself into doing what I can't do properly. Even if I could manage the estate, the daily contact with the people would keep me in an emotional struggle trying to pull the past into the current affairs. As hard as it is to turn my back on so many things I've enjoyed, I have to leave and see what I can do. Maybe this's what growing up is all about."

It had been bitterly cold at his grandfather's funeral and during his stay in Green Bay. As the train carried him south, he could see they were leaving the snow behind. The cast iron stove at the end of the car gave a degree of comfort to the coach plus the odor of burning coal. He would remember the coach odor as a part of this sad trip.

Dan did not leave his musing until hunger brought him to the current day. He had not checked but he was sure Eva and Kitty had supplied him with all he would need to eat. He observed they were almost through North Carolina and traveling along the route he had taken on his walk home from Savannah. How much had happened in a little more than four years but then think about the four years before that. A way of life has been destroyed and some signs of a new life were beginning. At least, the train service was improving.

Dan got back to his job location in northern Mississippi and found his boss still wanted him on the job. They had years of work ahead of them in rebuilding the bridges and trestles which had been damaged during the war. Both the South and the North had taken turns destroying the roadbed at various stages of the war. Most of the country had been treated worse than the roadbed. This area between Corinth and Memphis had about as rough treatment as any area. The people were trying to get their lives redirected but it was a struggle and a poor country as far as Dan could see.

Dan continued his contacts with the nearest railroad agent. These people were a source of information about the people in the area and a supply of newspapers Dan could read on his day off. He was amazed to learn Senator Summers had engaged in a bitter attack on President Grant. Dan read this as a foolish try; Grant had more power to harm Summers than Summers had to harm Grant. Maybe Summers lost some of his abilities when he was caned by Brooks.

Dan thought the admission of Virginia's congressional delegation was a step in the right direction in January 1870 and Mississippi's delegation was admitted nearly a month later. Some thought the control by the army had put people in the delegation who should not be there. Dan took a longer look at the process; you had to start on the road back, even if it was not paved the way you would like it to be.

In March, 1871, Dan read that Summers had been turned out of his position on the foreign relations committee. In a way, you could feel sorry for the man as this will be a real blow to his ego. It seems it had to be when he went out of his way to attack Grant. The failure of his marriage and now the failure to hold enough respect from his colleagues to allow him to continue as chairman of the foreign relations committee could cause his death. How my grandfather Johns would have liked to see a radical time-serving politician get what should have been coming to him.

Dan continued his work on the bridge gang as they moved west. Most of the country was in miserable shape by prewar standards but some people were trying to join the new order. No one liked some things they had to do but they were becoming convinced the good old days were not coming back. Dan read about the great fire in Chicago in October and thought not all bad things are happening in the South.

Shortly after the turn of the year, their bridge crew moved to a location on the outskirts of Mt. Pleasant. Dan made contact with the station agent to pick up the local news and to have the agent save the papers for him. The agent was surprised to learn that anyone on the crew was interested in reading. The contacts led to the agent suggesting Dan might like to attend services at his church the next Sunday. They were having a church dinner after the morning service. Dan could remember the good food the ladies brought to the train when they were on their way out of Richmond and thought attendance might be a pleasant experience. The food at the camp was adequate but it lacked the touch common to home cooked meals.

The services were a surprise to Dan. The minister was a young man and not the overstuffed windbag type. As the agent was moving Dan to the line to get his food, a young woman touched Dan's sleeve and asked, "Aren't you Mr. Wootton?"

Dan answered yes, as he turned to see who addressed him. He did not recognize the young lady until she volunteered she had seen him at his aunt's house in Richmond. Then he remembered Mary Jane and the cookies and the pleasant interlude at his aunt Ethel's house. He remembered the young girl had addressed him as Mr. Wootton then and it was no less than the shock he now had in seeing how she had changed. He learned she was now seventeen and lived nearby on a farm. The day was a very enjoyable experience and Dan resolved he would remember February 4, 1872. He found, on repeated visits, Sunday was something he looked to for the balance of the week.

Dan was more and more intrigued with Mary Jane. He was now twenty-seven and she was only seventeen but they seemed naturally attracted to each other. The more he saw of her, the more sure he was she would make an ideal mate for him. He proposed and was happy she agreed. She suggested they clean a small house near her mother's house and use it until they found where they wanted to be. The two worked putting the house in order and getting the things they would need to start their home. Dan had not been so happy since his carefree days when he was hunting with Macon.

They were married in March and Dan was happier than he would have thought possible. Gone was the pain of his war service, his mother's and his grandfather's death. He could not contain his pleasure with the experience with Mary Jane whom he called Molly. He thought the experience he had before the battle at Gettysburg had been pleasant but love with Molly was on an entirely different level. Now he could understand the rapture others had talked about. There was no way anyone could have made him believe their relationship could be so pleasant or so much fun. He was so full of joy with Molly, he wanted to let others know how good she was but discreet to keep their intimate pleasures only to themselves.

He had taken a week off the bridge crew duties and it was painful to report back to work and leave Molly at their home. He found he could hitch a ride with the foreman into town and walk out to the farm each night and back each morning. This gave him the pleasure of Molly each night and his pay as a member of the bridge crew. He had not complained about the crew quarters in previous days but they were sad in comparison with the company and pleasure of Molly.

The spring and summer of 1872 always would be one of the delightful memorable periods for Dan and Molly. They enjoyed exploring the delights they found in each other and in getting the items they needed for their new life together. Dan's job on the bridge crew brought in hard money, not otherwise easy to come by in this part of the world. They and Molly's family were thrilled with the news the Woottons would have an addition sometime in January. Dan made plans to leave the bridge crew and to farm part of the property Molly's mother owned. The land had been idle since 1866 and looked like a great weed patch but Dan and Molly thought it gave great promise. They bought a brace of oxen and borrowed a plow and soon had the land prepared for the winter rains and spring planting. Molly was as tickled with her own garden plot as with the soon-to-be birth of her first child.

Molly delivered a baby girl on January 20 and she named the baby Ola. She had hoped it would be a boy to please Mr. Wootton, as she continued to refer to Dan. Dan was delighted and assured her there was plenty of time ahead to wish for a boy. Dan thought the baby looked like his mother and thought how much joy she would have had if she could have lived to see her grandchild.

Dan got to town at intervals and continued to pick up the papers from the station agent. He was alarmed at the rash of smallpox, yellow fever and cholera through the southern cities during the summer. How fortunate he and Molly were to live in the country. It might be dull by some standards but they enjoyed their new life together and their new daughter. Most of what they needed came from the garden or the farm. The papers were full of the scandals and the panic of 1873 but Dan's reaction was, "I don't have anything; the crisis barely will touch me."

Molly thought they had more than most people, their health, their daughter, their zest for life and all the fresh food they needed.

Neither Dan nor his in-laws tried to hire any of the Negroes. What ground they could not cultivate themselves, they let lie fallow. His in-laws thought the life they led was demeaning but better than putting up with the troubles people had trying to get the Negroes to work. Most people found they could not rely on the Negroes doing the work the way they thought it should be done. The Negroes thought they should be given a plot of land. They believed stories about owners dismissing Negroes before harvest time or using other means of cheating the Negroes out of their wages or share of the harvest. There was little trust or faith between the Negroes and the owners; little, if any, between the owners or the Negroes in their contacts with the Yankee occupation troops. War almost broke out when a Negro cavalry troop was stationed in Mt. Pleasant. Dan had a trying session with a group that met after the Sunday services. They wanted to make an armed response. Dan made the point, the war is over and we have been defeated. That does not make it right but the damn-Yankees have the means to do what they wish to do. Any armed response will only bring more trouble to our area. Most of the group thought there should be some way they could retaliate but for the time being, they would think about the problem.

Dan had been corresponding with the attorney Wootton trying to get him to settle the Johns' estate. His grandfather had been blinded by his obsession with blocking his son-in-law from getting any benefit from the Johns' estate. The result was he had left a loop-hole for the attorney to manipulate the estate. The only money the attorney got from the estate was a seven percent fee for any transaction. There was no incentive for him to settle the estate when he got nothing for the act but could get a fee on any profit, sale or trade he could make. After a series of letters brought no action, Dan hired an attorney in Farmville to sue to force the estate to be settled. Dan's attorney notified him that attorney Wootton had obtained a postponement when the matter had been set for hearing. Dan's attorney wanted an additional fee to follow the matter and after several such postponements and fees, Dan decided he was only wasting the little money he and Molly had. His father wrote him in late 1873 that attorney Wootton was becoming a major land holder. Dan understood the attorney was set on milking the Johns estate until it fell into his lap. It had been a fortune once; a large part had disappeared during and after the war and now it appeared the land value was being downgraded.

There is a lesson to be gained from this thought Dan, "Molly and I are lucky to have our health and know how to work to make our own living. Maybe we couldn't have received any greater gift; whatever we have will be what we do for ourselves. We don't have to worry about the good old days, just do what we can. We are a lot better off than many of our acquaintances who can only hope the good old days will return."

On one of his trips into town to pick up papers from the agent, he found a letter from Macon. His mother, he said, had told him where Dan was. He wanted to know how conditions were in Dan's area. It looked like he would have to move to some other location. As much as he had enjoyed his life in Savannah, current conditions were far from good. A white man had put a pistol to Macon's head and taken his boat. The excuse being no Negro had a right to own a business like Macon had. He had tried to get a hearing but all he got was threats of violence if he pressed for the return of the boat. He and his wife's family thought they would be better off in some other location. His mother did not think western Virginia offered any promise.

Dan thought, "Macon didn't deserve to be treated that way but he's lucky the fellow didn't kill him and take his boat. With the coming election, there is no telling what will be happening here. For sure, it'll not be good for the Confederate veterans and maybe not for anyone who isn't on the inside. For us, the invitation to follow our friends to Texas looks better all the time. Molly wouldn't like to leave her mother. Her mother and step-father wouldn't leave. They couldn't sell their land for anything near its value but we don't have anything to lose by leaving and maybe something to gain if we do go. I wish there was something I could do to help Macon, he's a good man and deserves better than what he is getting. Maybe we all do. These are not good days for most people. Maybe we'll someday learn how to have honest good government but the moment seems to be taken by crooks and wild dreamers at both the state and national level. The best hope seems to be for the pigs to root in the trough hard enough to start a fight among themselves. It's a shame to have nothing better to tell Macon other than a dream life may be better in Texas."

The election put General Ames in as governor with a black man, A. K. Davis, as lieutenant governor. The blacks remembered General Ames for the things he did to support their cause when he was military governor. They got two other blacks on the ticket. The new government took over on January 22, 1874. General Ames started on a program to reduce state expenses. No one could believe the Republicans would start the trend. They were the ones who increased taxes to fourteen times what they had been. It sounded better than what they thought they might hear. Dan and the rest of their friends at church worried more about the blacks who went into office with General Ames. The general had never been able to take the summers in Mississippi and had always gone back to Ohio for a month or two to escape the heat. If he continued this practice and everyone thought he would, the state would be left in the hands of Lt. Governor Davis. No one had any doubts that the results from Davis would be worse than what they would get from General Ames.

Early March turned cold, as though the weather was putting on one last breath of winter before jumping into the summer heat. Dan and Molly used to laugh at the idea that if you didn't look carefully, you might miss spring and go from winter straight to summer. Dan put Molly and the baby in the ox cart and the three of them went to town on Saturday, March 7. It gave Molly a chance to visit with the pastor's wife, while Dan talked to the agent and picked up the newspapers. Molly asked the pastor's wife if she didn't think Dan looked good in his uniform jacket as they watched him walk to the depot. Molly said the jacket was the only good warm thing Dan had and he would wear it when he wanted to look his best.

The two women had just begun to enjoy the fireplace and a cup of hot chocolate when Dan returned. He was very upset and his jacket coat was hanging open. He explained he had been stopped by a squad of cavalry and the Negro lieutenant had cut the buttons off his jacket with his saber. The pastor's wife said she would get the pastor to protest the outrage to the sheriff. Dan asked for her not do that. The whole bunch had been drinking and thought they would have a little fun. "I'll have to decide what I'll do about it." The pastor's wife wanted him to take off his jacket and she would sew buttons on it. Dan thanked her, but said, "I want it left as it is but I'll borrow a safety pin if I may."

There was a long silence as the three of them made their way back to the farm. Molly and the baby pulled the blanket tight to ward off the cold. She was shocked that anyone would do such a thing to Mr. Wootton. She could remember the horror and misery the Yankees caused at her mother's place during the war. They had taken all the horses and what stock they did not take they ruined by cutting their tongues. A trooper had been rummaging through the house looking for loot when he discharged his pistol. Her mother's aunt died from the shock. After the troopers had left and her mother had looked over the damage they had done, she caught a mule and rode to General Sherman's camp. Everyone tried to stop her as she got to the camp but she insisted she was going to see the General. Her reply to every challenge was either I see the General or you'll have to shoot me. The general heard her story and dispatched his orderly to help put the place back in enough order for them to survive. The troopers buried the aunt and put some order back into the premises. There was not much anyone could do about the utter destruction war makes. Before General Sherman left the area they had been supplied with bacon and hardtack so they would not starve. The crowning gesture was half a sack of coffee beans the general delivered by his orderly. She would agree with Mr. Wootton those people were damn-Yankees but she would never be able to tell him one of them, General Sherman, was a gentleman.

CHAPTER XVII

Gone to Texas

*T*HE evening meal was as quiet as the trip back from town. Molly thought it better not to talk about anything since she thought Mr. Wootton was weighing options. When he got to a point where he has the problem in focus, he would break the silence. The night stayed cold. Shortly after they got into bed, the baby began to fuss. Molly gathered the baby up and brought her to bed with them. She seemed to be contented when the three of them snuggled together to keep out the night chill. Molly thought this is how it shall be; the three of us as one and we will be comfortable.

The morning broke bright and clear with a hint the cold weather would be gone by the day's end. Dan suggested they have the day to themselves instead of their usual Sunday practice of church and dinner with the congregation. He finished his chores with the animals and returned to watch Molly prepare their dinner and care for the baby. The baby still looked like a small copy of his mother.

After dinner, Dan said, "Let me hold the baby, while you wash the dishes and then we can talk about what we should do." Dan began by saying, "It's pleasant to live near your mother and to enjoy our church. Some of our friends have gone to Texas and write back about the land and life they think is better than what they had here. General Ames is unlikely to make life better for us here and there is the problem of what to do about the Negro who publicly humiliated me. It would be easy enough to kill him.

"I have my grandfather's rifle, shotgun and pistol. Whether I kill him or not, the probable result is someone will. I'll be one of the suspects but the real killer may be one of his own troopers if what I hear about his night-time affairs is near the truth. I have done enough killing in the army and I want to put that life behind me. Getting rid of him would make a small part of me think I had righted a wrong but it really would not solve anything. I think we'll have a better life with a fresh start. Think about it and if you agree, we need to tell your family and get organized for the trip to Milam County, Texas. It looks like we'll have a break in the weather if we get ready to leave on Monday the 16th. We can tell everyone good-by at church next Sunday. Your folks may or may not want to join us now or come after we get settled. From what I hear, we may be near Rockdale but it could be Thorndale or San Gabriel or anywhere in the triangle."

Molly replied, "I decided last night when I put the baby in bed with us; we would always be as one. I'll tell mother today and start thinking about what to pack and take with us."

Dan said, "Great and I'll make sure the oxen and the cart are ready to take us to Texas within the week. We'll not make many miles each day but the oxen are dependable. I'll take my carpenter tools and my guns. I don't have much else except a little gold that I have left from my bridge work. We'll have to plan where we carry it and the other things we want to take with us. We'll hate to part with anything we have used to make our home. The rocker your mother gave you is a problem to take but you love it and I like to see the contented look on your face when you rock the baby, so we'll have to take it. We may have problems parting with other things; maybe it is a blessing we do not have too much. If we had been here for years, we would have so many painful decisions to make we couldn't leave."

Dan awoke the next morning with a new vigor. It's amazing, he thought, how a decision on what course of action to take puts a spur to your activity. He went over the things he had to do before they left. Pull and oil the wheels on the ox cart, check the tongue and yoke, and check the animals. He would have to plan where to locate things on the cart based on what they would need each day and what they would not need until they got to Texas. His carpentry tools would not be needed until the got to their new home; they could be fitted in under what they would need each day. His guns, he hoped, would not be needed but they should be carried where he could get to them. Not everyone on the road could be counted on to be friendly or honest. He decided he would make a false bottom for the cradle he had made for the baby and there he would carry the few pieces of gold. He would need more rope and tarpaulins to secure the load. The tarpaulins would protect Molly and the baby from the occasional showers including keeping their bedding and blankets dry. Their little stove had been a center of their domestic life but he did not see how they could take it with them. They would start with ample fresh food and in a few days they would have to use dry foods, hardtack and bacon. They would have to snack for their noon meal and stop early enough each day to cook and wash. Going now should give about the best break in the weather we'll get. There should be forage for the animals along the way.

Molly's family came by to take the three of them to church on Sunday, March 15. Molly's mother claimed her rights to hold Ola, her first grandchild. The weather had turned bright, clear and balmy. Their family was the center of attention at the services and at the church dinner afterwards. They had a warm and friendly day with their friends with many promises to write and tell them about their new life. Several of their friends wanted to leave with them but had to stay to care for their parents. Molly's mother made them promise to come to her house for supper and to stop for breakfast as they left the next morning.

Several members had, during the week, tried to engage Dan in a scheme to "take care of the uppity lieutenant." Dan had assured them he was capable and willing to do the job alone but he had decided not to do it. His judgment had been and still was that someone would do it. He did not want them to be at risk over the affair. The best course for everyone, he thought, was to keep the affair quiet and hope the lieutenant stayed healthy until sometime after March 16.

Monday's daylight woke Dan and he stretched to enjoy the comfort of their bed. He had the cart packed except for their bed, the cradle and the rocking chair. He had made boxes for their dishes and supplies. The boxes made a seat for Molly near the front of the cart and a space between those boxes and his tool chest made a space for his guns. Their bedding and a tarpaulin would provide cover but leave the guns within easy reach if they were needed. Molly dressed herself and the baby, while Dan tied on the cradle and the rocking chair. Then they were off on their trip with the stop after the first half mile at her mother's house for breakfast.

Their breakfast brought back memories of the hunting trips Dan used to take with his grandfather Johns. Eva used to always see they started with steak and eggs. Molly's mother wanted them to have a good send-off. The steak and eggs with hot biscuit and gravy and good coffee were her way of saying, "We love you and hate to see you go but have a good trip." Dan and Molly made their individual good-byes to the family and were off on their adventure. They waved as they made the turn into the road and then never looked back. The canvas water-bags hanging from the cart waved back to the family as the cart movement made them rock from side to side.

The third day out, they crossed the Mississippi. Someone had told Molly if you washed your face in the river the first time you crossed it, you would cross it again. She tried to get Dan to wash his face with the river water but he said, "There is nothing to make me want to come back."

While they were waiting for the ferry, she went to the river and washed her face and the baby's. She did not know if it would do any good but she wanted to return.

Their trip became a routine of early morning breakfast by the campfire and on the road until early evening when they would make camp. Molly soon got the cooking chores down to a routine. They sometimes had small game Dan shot as they passed through the countryside and were occasionally lucky enough to get fresh vegetables. She made good use of a cast iron pot and lid her mother had given them. She could cover it with coals and tend to other chores, while the evening meal was cooking. Dan made a routine of seeing that the oxen had water and grazing and checking them and the cart for signs of what would need attention.

Molly worried about Mr. Wootton walking each day, while she and the baby rode. Dan said, "If I could do the walking that I did on the way into Pennsylvania and then from Savannah to Virginia, I can do this trip. For sure, my leg isn't as good as it was on the Pennsylvania walk but I don't have to carry a heavy pack. I need to be on the ground to control the oxen and I have done heavier work on the bridge crew. We should be thankful we have our health and be happy to do what we want to do. This type of good luck does not come to everyone."

Dan did not see much land in Arkansas or east Texas that interested him. As they got further into Texas, he thought the countryside looked better. The rolling landscape and occasional streams or creeks appealed to him. It did not strike him why he liked what he saw until about the time he got to Rockdale. Then it dawned on him it looked like his home in Virginia but with land which appeared to be more productive. They found their friends living south of Rockdale about two miles.

They visited with their friends and the next day went with them to look at a small place. Their friends thought it would be available for rent. They found the bridge washed out and a small creek had to be forded to get to the property. Their friends thought the washed-out bridge was the reason the place was still for rent. The house was small but there was wood and water and plenty of land for their needs. Over the weekend, they made contact with the owner and rented the place with the owner agreeing to pay for the bridge replacement materials if Dan would build the bridge.

Dan and Molly could not wait to get started on getting their new home into being. Molly left the baby with their friends; she and Dan waded the creek to get to the house. They cleaned the house, checked the well and made a temporary crossing. They returned tired from the physical work but thrilled with the progress they had made. They enjoyed the move-in the next day; it was starting their married life over. Dan prepared a planting area for Molly's garden, turned to plowing the field for their crops and then to the work of rebuilding the bridge.

Within a week, they felt like they were the most lucky people. They had made the trip without disaster, had better land to work than they had in Mississippi, friends nearby and an introduction to a new church group. Soon, word got around about Dan's skill as a carpenter and he began to get offers to use his skills to build other bridges. His wish to trade his carpentry work for items they needed found a ready market. Money was hard to come by but produce, livestock and farm tools were readily available. His carpenter's tool box proved to be the resource that brought them pigs, chickens and a plow.

By the fall of 1874, they felt the move had been good for them. After harvesting his corn and fodder crops, Dan went to work on a large barn and corral for one of the nearby land owners. The return for his efforts was a runabout and a horse. Molly and Dan were delighted. It surely was not a stylish carriage but to them it was a signal life was better here and they were in the stream to improve their lot. No longer would they have to walk or use the ox cart for church or visiting their friends.

Near the end of the year, Dan received word his father had died. Thomas Ballard Wootton had lived on the charity of his relatives for several years. Dan felt sorry for him but in his father's troubled world, maybe sixty-one years was a lifetime. His father's father had lived beyond eighty years.

They looked to 1875 with bright hope. Molly told Dan she thought she was pregnant. If she was right, they would have a second child in July. In February, the estate of his grandfather Johns was distributed to Dan and his sister and brothers. Dan thought $150 was a pittance as compared to what he should have received but he thought this and the war experience is good to put behind me. That life is gone and it is not coming back; it is better to put those matters aside. We cannot gain anything by going over those times and experiences; we now have to build a new life.

The new Thomas Ballard Wootton was born in July. Dan thought they should keep the name alive but he was going to do his best to see this fellow walked a different path. He and Molly were both delighted their second child was a boy. They were equally happy watching the two-year-old, Ola, toddle about exploring and expanding the limits of her world. There was not much of anything she would not try. During the rainy season, several people observed the bridges Dan had built did not wash out. This brought more attention to Dan's skill as a carpenter.

The election year of 1876 brought several surprises to Dan. The first was the news about the Custer massacre at Bighorn in late June. Dan had heard during the war that this fellow was a rash soldier. He had been more lucky than smart then and this time his luck did not hold.

In the fall, there was more interest in southern voting than there had been since the war. There were spirited rallies and contested dual slates in several states. Tilden won the popular vote but not the electoral vote. The bitter contest over votes in four states brought the election to the House of Representatives. There were moments when it looked as though civil war would breakout again. Congress appointed a committee of fifteen (eight Republicans, seven Democrats) to see if a comprise could be obtained. The Republicans were so anxious to stay in power for another four years they were willing to agree to having a southerner in the cabinet, to share patronage with local politicians, and to withdraw Federal troops from the south. The Republicans got a verbal promise the Negroes would be fairly treated; the Democrats got a written and signed agreement from Hayes. Dan thought the southern people got the best of this bargaining. As it later developed, the Republicans were unhappy with Hayes. Most of the bitterness seemed to be directed at Mrs. Hayes who would not let any spirits be served at White House functions. The term "lemonade Lucy" became a symbol of what politicians looked upon as the dull and dry four years of the Hayes administration.

By mid-year 1877, they were surprised by the appearance of Dan's younger brother, Freemont Wootton. Dan was glad to see his seventeen-year-old brother but did not believe his casual story about the reason for the visit. He let the story stand, thinking the true story will come out, whenever he thinks he can trust me. One day as they were working in the field, Freemont suggested they take a break and cool off in the creek.

After they were in the water, Freemont said, "There's something I want to talk about. The reason I'm here is they trusted me to take some horses into Richmond to get some money for the spring plantings. The damn-Yankees were buying horses and this was the most probable way to get gold to pay for the seed and the help to produce the crop. I made the sale and started back home on my pony when I saw a game where the fellow had three shells and one pea. As I sat on my pony and watched the game, the fellow playing was losing nearly every time but I knew where the pea was every time. After a little while, the man asked if I wanted to play. It seemed I could not help but win and to think how proud they would be when I brought home the extra money. Well you know what happened. I couldn't go home and tell them what a dummy I'd been. It was the worst thing I could imagine. The only thing I could think to do was to try to get to Texas and hope I could find you."

No wonder this kid has been so up tight. Dan said, "Let's see if we can talk this out. You lost all the gold that you got for the horses?"

"Yes. I kept thinking my luck would turn."

"How did you live on the way down here?"

"I worked and begged for food for my horse and myself."

"Well, one thing we can learn is if something looks too good to be true, it probably is. How many horses did you take into Richmond?"

"Fifteen."

"The second thing then appears true. There's no way you or I can get our hands on money in that amount. I make a living for us on the land and get some work as a carpenter but the pay is nearly always in trade for something we need. Hard money is difficult to come by here. There's a major distrust of banks in this state and the recent war didn't improve things. I think we should let my uncle know you are here with me and why you got to this spot. Beyond that step, there isn't anything you or I can do to improve their lot. We should treat it like I do the war, leave it alone, it's behind us and we have to look to the future. Do you have any idea what you would like to do?"

"Not really. I don't think I'm made to do as you do. Farming always seems boring to me and a waste of time though it is a way of putting food on the table. There must be something I can do that would be more to my liking. If the damn-Yankees were buying horses, maybe I should see if I would make it in the cavalry. What do you think?"

"That's one option. It lands you in a berth, gives you something you know you can do and will give you some money. Let's leave it for the time being. You can help me here and maybe some other thing will turn up. Does that sound right to you?"

"I think it would be great. You know I think your kids are much fun and I like to play with them. Molly, I think, is a real gem. If I ever cause you a problem, let me know and I'll move. I'll always be grateful to you for the kind treatment you have given me."

Dan told Molly what he had learned and the decisions they had made when he could talk without Free overhearing their conversation. He asked Molly not to disclose to Free she was privy to the reason for his visit. He admitted Free enlisting with the damn-Yankees was not the most pleasant thing but at the moment he had no better suggestion. The boy needs time before he can do anything but worry about the foolish thing he did and he's still a boy. He has much growing to do. I guess I was the same at his age but I was already in the army and it does something to you.

Life continued on the same plane for the five in the household for several months. Molly got Dan's ear one night to explain to him she thought it was time for Free to move on. She heard him teaching bawdy songs to the kids which was just another sign Free was not in tune with their life. He was a good kid but bored and needed to find himself.

The next day, Dan suggested they try their hands at fishing in the creek. Molly said she would make them a lunch but she thought she would not go. It would be too much work to try to keep the two kids out of the creek and poison ivy. While they were fishing, Dan told Free that try as he had, he could not come up with anything better for him to do than to see if he liked the cavalry.

Free said, "It's my judgment, too. I think I'll ride on down to San Antonio and see what they say."

Several weeks later, they got a note from Free thanking them for their kindness to him. When he got to San Antonio, he went to the post and tried to enlist.

The Sergeant asked him how old he was and Free told him, eighteen. The Sergeant said, "Come back in the afternoon and maybe you will be twenty-one."

Free said, "I did and I was. I think we'll be based on the border. Will let you know when I know more."

Dan and Molly hoped he would be happy. They did not know anything better for him. They were happy and content and wished for others the same love in life.

CHAPTER XVIII

Summary, 1917

"MOLLY, if you have time sit and reminisce with me. It's now 1917 and you and I'll have been married forty-five years next month. It'll soon be fifty-six years since I fed you cookies at Aunt Ethel's house in Richmond. Think of all the things we have been through. It's amazing to me; I could have been killed in the war, died of camp fever, lost my leg at Gettysburg, never found you except from the luck of helping the old man build the bridge for the army in 1862. How could we have had nine children and raised seven without the trouble other people have had and still have our health. Sadie, our last one, I guess will marry the Montague boy. He seems to be a good lad. That will leave us alone here on our little plot of land at the edge of Rockdale. Eleven acres does not compare with what my grandfather owned but this patch seems to give us enough. Ola is married to Basil Smith, one of the best farmers in the area and they have a fine family. Tom is a successful contractor near Dallas, Evie and her family are nearby, the same for Taylor. We surely are not going to run out of grandchildren. Bertie has married the Clark fellow and they have the one daughter; never thought I would stand for one of mine marrying a damn-Yankee. We must be getting mellow in our old age."

"What I heard about you in town last week, does not sound like you have mellowed much, Mr. Wootton."

"I do not know what you are talking about."

"Were you in the crowd gathered around the wagon when the preacher was telling about the love of Jesus Christ."

"Oh, that. Well, he went too far. I was with him all the way until he turned and asked me to confirm that Christ's love could make a Confederate love a Yankee. I had to slam my hat and disagree with him. Who told you about that, anyway?"

"I overheard people talking about it in the store. I do not know who they were."

"We have had a long life, especially me. I think it natural as we look back to think maybe we should have taken a different path. It may have been better for us and there is an equal chance it could have been worse. It still is a wonder to me I wasn't killed in the war and a greater mystery that if I hadn't enlisted when I did, I might not have had cookies with you when you and your mother were in Richmond. There is never anything to be gained by worrying about what might have been. These people who try to embellish the glorious south make me sick. There is nothing to be gained; it's past. Let it go; put it behind you. The life we have is now and the little time we'll have of the future.

"One of the things I thought we would do for our children was to see they studied Greek and Latin. I guess I thought they should because my parents were so determined I should do it. My father thought no one could be anything in this world unless he knew Greek and Latin. Our kids seem to be doing all right and so did we but I somehow wish they had the lessons. This may be minor because they are well and happy.

"It looks as though we may get into the current war in Europe, despite Wilson's promise. I don't think it'll cure anything any more than the war between the states did. The human race may make some progress from generation to generation but it seems to be in mechanical things; our ability to understand the other fellow and make a better world does not seem to make the progress it should.

"That was a good thing for Madie to ride the train back from the west to visit us and let us get acquainted with her first one. He watched everything I did and seemed to enjoy being with me. The fellows at the ice plant gave him a sliver of ice every day. Incidentally, you were right about him. He is different.

"I guess life is easier for us now but I remember the good times we had after Macon brought Kitty and his family out to be near us. Remember how I always bought them a keg of beer after the harvest season. When Kitty thought they had enough, she would up-end the keg and sit on it. The whole group would then try to sing Kitty to sleep. We used to enjoy walking down to their cabin and listen to their singing as we stood outside in the dark. Maybe there are greater concerts but none better we have heard. There are so many great memories I have of our life together.

"I hope we have many more years together. You have been and still are a great companion in every way. I'm sure you know when I do leave you, I want to go in my old Confederate jacket with the safety pins instead of buttons."